Her gaze connected to the most gorgeous pair of hazel eyes.

At that moment Crystal knew it *was* Bane. She was about to open the door when she remembered the note. *Trust no one.* But this wasn't just anyone. This was Bane.

She unlocked the door and stepped back. Soft porch light poured into her foyer as Bane stepped in. He'd always been tall, but the man entering her house appeared a lot taller than she remembered. And he was no longer slender. He was all muscles, perfectly proportioned to his height and weight. And when her gaze settled on his face, she drew in a sharp breath. He even looked different. Rougher. Tougher.

He closed the door behind him and her heart pounded. A part of her wanted to race to him, tell him how glad she was to see him, how much she had missed him, but she couldn't. Her legs refused to move and she knew why.

For some reason this Bane was like a stranger to her. Had five years of separation done that to them?

* * *

Bane is part of *New York Times* bestselling author Brenda Jackson's The Westmorelands series: a family bound by loyalty...and love!

Dear Reader,

When I first introduced the Westmoreland family, little did I know they would have such a huge impact on your lives. Originally, the Westmoreland family series consisted of one core group—Delaney and her five brothers: Dare, Thorn, Stone, Storm and Chase. Then there were the cousins—Jared, Spencer, Durango, Ian, Quade and Reggie. Lastly, there were Uncle Corey's triplets—Clint, Cole and Casey.

I soon discovered more cousins living in Denver and they became known as the Denver Westmorelands. That meant my readers got to know even more Westmorelands. I believe that of all the Westmorelands I have introduced to my readers, none has captured my readers' hearts and imaginations more than Brisbane "Bane" Westmoreland, the youngest male Westmoreland of them all.

From the introduction of the Denver Westmorelands, Bane was known as a hotheaded troublemaker and a young man totally obsessed with a young woman by the name of Crystal Newsome. Now that Bane's book has finally come around, Bane has become a disciplined military man who is still obsessed with his Crystal.

Bane is Brisbane and Crystal's story. And I hope all of you enjoy reading it as much as I enjoyed writing it.

Happy reading!

Brenda Jackson

BANE

BRENDA JACKSON

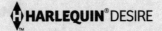

HARLEQUIN® DESIRE

Recycling programs
for this product may
not exist in your area.

ISBN-13: 978-0-373-73426-9

Bane

Printed in U.S.A.

www.Harlequin.com

Brenda Jackson is a *New York Times* bestselling author of more than one hundred romance titles. Brenda lives in Jacksonville, Florida, and divides her time between family, writing and traveling.

Email Brenda at authorbrendajackson@gmail.com or visit her on her website at brendajackson.net.

Books by Brenda Jackson

Harlequin Desire

Visit her Author Profile page at Harlequin.com, or brendajackson.net, for more titles!

To the man who will always and forever be the love of my life, Gerald Jackson, Sr.

So then, my beloved brethren, let every man be swift to hear, slow to speak, slow to wrath.
—*James* 1:19

Prologue

"You wanted to see me, Dil?" Brisbane Westmoreland asked, walking into his eldest brother Dillon's home office.

The scenic view out the window was that of Gemma Lake, the main waterway that ran through the rural part of Denver the locals referred to as Westmoreland Country. For Bane, this was home. This wasn't Afghanistan, Iraq or Syria, which meant he didn't have to worry about booby traps, enemies hiding behind trees and bushes or the boat dock being wired with explosives set to go off the second someone stepped on it. Westmoreland Country was a place where he felt safe. All in all, he was glad to be back home.

Thanksgiving dinner had ended hours ago, and keeping with family traditions, everyone had gathered outside for a game of snow volleyball. Now the females in the Westmoreland family had gathered in the sitting room to watch a holiday movie with the kids, and the men had gone upstairs for a card game.

"Yes, come on in, Bane."

Bane stopped in front of Dillon's desk. He knew Dillon was studying him with that sharp eye of his, taking in every detail. And he could imagine what his brother was thinking. Bane was not the same habitual troublemaker who had left Westmoreland Country five years ago to make something of himself.

Bane would be the first to admit that a lot in his life had changed. He was now military through and through, both mentally as well as physically. Since graduating from the naval academy and becoming a navy SEAL, he'd learned a lot, seen a lot and done a lot…all in the name of the United States government.

"I want to know how you're doing," Dillon inquired, interrupting Bane's thoughts.

Bane drew in a deep breath. He wished he could answer truthfully. Under normal circumstances he would say he was in prime fighting condition, but that was not the case. During his team's last covert operation, an enemy's bullet had nearly taken him out, leaving him flat on his back in a hospital bed for nearly two months. But he couldn't tell Dillon that. It was confidential. So he said, "I'm fine, although my last mission took a toll on me. I lost a team member who was also a good friend."

Dillon shook his head sadly. "I'm sorry to hear that."

"Me, too. Laramie Cooper was a good guy. One of the best. We went through the academy together." Bane knew Dillon wouldn't ask for specifics. Bane had explained to his family early on that all his covert ops were classified and linked to national security and couldn't be discussed.

Dillon didn't say anything for a minute and then he

asked, "Is that why you're taking a three-month military leave? Because of your friend's death?"

Bane eased down in the leather armchair across from Dillon's desk. When their parents, aunt and uncle had gotten killed in a plane crash over twenty years ago, Dillon, the eldest of the Denver Westmorelands, had acquired the role of guardian of his six brothers—Micah, Jason, Riley, Stern, Canyon and Bane—and his eight cousins—Ramsey, Zane, Derringer, Megan, Gemma, the twins Adrian and Aidan, and Bailey. As far as Bane was concerned Dillon had done an outstanding job in keeping the family together and making sure they each made something of themselves. All while making Blue Ridge Land Management Corporation, founded by their father and uncle, into a Fortune 500 company.

Since Dillon was the eldest, he had inherited the main house in Westmoreland Country along with the three hundred acres it sat on. Everyone else, upon reaching the age of twenty-five, received one hundred acres to call their own. Thanks to Bailey's creative mind, each of their spreads were given names—Ramsey's Web, Zane's Hideout, Derringer's Dungeon, Megan's Meadows, Gemma's Gem, Jason's Place, Stern's Stronghold, Canyon's Bluff and Bane's Ponderosa. It was beautiful land that encompassed mountains, valleys, lakes, rivers and streams.

Again, Bane thought about how good it was to be home, and safe here talking with his brother.

"No, that's not the reason," Bane said. "All my team members are on leave because our last operation was one from hell. However, I'm using my leave for a specific purpose, and that is to find Crystal."

Bane paused before adding somberly, "If nothing

else, Coop's death showed me how fragile life is. You can be here today and gone tomorrow."

Dillon would never know that Bane wasn't just referring to Coop's life, but also how close he'd come to losing his own more than a few times.

Bane watched as Dillon came around and sat on the edge of his desk to face him, unsure of how his brother had taken what he'd just said about finding Crystal. Especially since she was the main reason Dillon, and the rest of Bane's family, had supported his decision to join the navy. During their teen years, Bane and Crystal had been obsessive about each other in a way that had driven her family, as well as his, out of their wits.

"Like I told you when you came home for Jason's wedding…" Dillon said. "When the Newsomes moved away they didn't leave a forwarding address. I think their main objective was to put as much distance between you and Crystal as they could." He paused, then said, "But after your inquiry, I hired a private investigator to locate their whereabouts, and I'm not sure if you know it but Carl Newsome passed away."

Bane shook his head. Although he definitely hadn't been Mr. Newsome's favorite person, the man had been Crystal's father. She and her dad hadn't always seen eye to eye, but Crystal had loved him nonetheless. "No, I didn't know he had died."

Dillon nodded. "I called and spoke to Emily Newsome, who told me about Carl's death from lung cancer. After offering my condolences, I asked about Crystal. She said Crystal was doing fine, working on her master's degree at Harvard with plans to get a PhD in biochemistry from there, as well."

Bane tipped his head to the side. "That doesn't surprise me. Crystal was pretty smart. If you recall she was two grades ahead and was set to graduate from high school at sixteen."

What he wouldn't bring up was that she would have done just that if she hadn't missed so many days of school playing hooky with him. That was something everyone, especially the Newsomes, blamed him for. Whenever Crystal had attended school steadily she'd made good grades. There was no doubt in his mind she would have graduated at the top of her class. That was one of the reasons he hadn't tried to find her for all these years. He'd wanted her to reach her full potential. He'd owed her that much.

"So you haven't seen or heard from Crystal since that day Carl sent her to live with some aunt?"

"No, I haven't seen her. You were right at the time. I didn't have anything to offer Crystal. I was a hothead and Trouble was my middle name. She deserved better and I was willing to make something of myself to give her better."

Dillon just stared at him for a long moment in silence, as if contemplating whether or not he should tell him something. Bane suddenly felt uneasy. Had something happened to Crystal that he didn't know about?

"Is there something else, Dil?"

"I don't want to hurt or upset you Bane, but I want to give you food for thought. You're planning to find Crystal, but you don't know what her feelings are for you now. The two of you were young. First love doesn't always mean last love. Although you might still care about her, for all you know she might have moved on, gotten on with her life without you. It's been five years. Have you considered that she might be involved with someone else?"

Bane leaned back in his chair, considering Dillon's

words. "I don't believe that. Crystal and I had an understanding. We have an unbreakable bond."

"But that was years ago," Dillon stressed. "You just said you haven't seen her since that day Carl sent her away. For all you know she could be married by now."

Bane shook his head. "Crystal wouldn't marry anyone else."

Dillon lifted a brow. "And how can you be so sure of that?"

Bane held his brother's stare. "Because she's already married, Dil. Crystal is married to me and I think it's time to go claim my wife."

Dillon was on his feet in a flash. "Married? You? Crystal? B-but how? When?"

"When we eloped."

"But you and Crystal never made it to Vegas."

"Weren't trying to," Bane said evenly. "We deliberately gave that impression to send everyone looking for us in the wrong direction. We got married in Utah."

"Utah? You have to be eighteen to marry without parental consent and Crystal was seventeen."

Bane shook his head. "She was seventeen the day we eloped, but turned eighteen the next day."

Dillon stared at him. "Then, why didn't the two of you say something? Why didn't she tell her parents that she was your wife or why didn't you tell us? You let them send her away."

"Yes, because I knew that although she was my wife, I could still be brought up on kidnapping charges. I violated the restraining order from that judge when I set foot on her parents' property. If you recall, Judge Foster was pissed about it and wanted to send me to the prison farm for a year. And knowing Mr. Newsome, had I mentioned anything about me and Crystal being married, he would have demanded that Judge Foster send me away for even longer. Once I was gone, Newsome would have found a way to have our marriage annulled or forced Crystal into divorcing me. She and I both knew that so we decided not to say anything about our marriage no matter what…even if it meant being apart for a short while."

"A short while? You've been apart for five years."

"I hadn't planned for it to be this long. We figured her old man would keep her under lock and key for a while. We were prepared for that seven-month separation because it would give Crystal a chance to finish high school. We hadn't figured on him sending her away. But then something you said that day stuck with me. At the time I had nothing to offer Crystal. She was smart and deserved more than a dumb ass who enjoyed being the town's troublemaker."

Bane didn't say anything for a minute before adding, "I told you earlier that I hadn't seen Crystal, but what I didn't say is that I managed to talk to her after she left town."

Dillon frowned. "You made contact with Crystal?"

"Only once. A few months after she was sent away."

"But how? Her parents made sure no one knew where she'd gone."

"Bailey found out for me."

Dillon shook his head. "Now, why doesn't that surprise me? And how did Bailey find out where Crystal was?"

Bane held his brother's gaze. "Are you sure you want to know?"

Dillon rubbed his hand down his face. "Does it involve breaking the law?"

Bane shrugged his shoulders. "Sort of."

Bailey was their female cousin who was a couple of years younger than Bane and the baby in the Denver Westmoreland family. While growing up, the two of them, along with the twins, Adrian and Aidan, had been extremely close, thick as thieves, literally. The four used to get into all kinds of trouble with the law. Bane knew that Dillon's close friendship with Sheriff Harper was what had kept them out of jail.

Now the twins were Harvard graduates. Adrian had a PhD in engineering and Aidan was a cardiologist at Johns Hopkins Research Hospital. And both were happily married. Bailey, who had her MBA, was marrying Walker Rafferty, a rancher from Alaska, on Valentine's Day and moving to live on his spread. That announcement had definitely come as a shock to Bane and everyone else since Bailey had always sworn she would never, ever leave Westmoreland Country. Bane had met Rafferty today and immediately liked the ex-marine. Bane had a feeling Rafferty would not only handle Bailey but would make Bane's cousin happy.

"So if you knew where she was, what stopped you from going to her?" Dillon asked, holding Bane's gaze.

"I didn't know where she was and I made Bailey promise not to tell me. I just needed to talk to her and Bailey arranged a call between me and Crystal that lasted about twenty minutes. I told her about my decision to join the navy and I made her a promise that while we were apart I would honor our marriage vows, and for her to always believe that one day I would come back for her. That was the last time we talked to each other."

Bane remembered that phone call as if it had been yesterday. "Another reason I needed to talk to Crystal was to be certain she hadn't gotten pregnant during the time we eloped. A pregnancy would have been a game changer for me. I would not have gone into the navy. Instead, I would have gone to her immediately."

Dillon nodded. "Do you know where she is now?"

"I didn't know up until a few hours ago. Bailey lost contact with Crystal a year and a half ago. Last week I hired someone to find her, and I got a call that she's been found. I'm heading out in the morning."

"To where?"

"Dallas, Texas."

One

Leaving her job at Seton Industries, Crystal Newsome quickly walked to her car, looking over her shoulder when she thought she heard footsteps behind her. She tried ignoring the sparks that moved up her arms, while telling herself she was probably getting all worked up for nothing. And all because of that note someone had left today in her desk drawer.

Someone wants the research you're working on. I suggest you disappear for a while. No matter what, don't trust anyone.

After reading it she had glanced around the lab. Her four colleagues seemed preoccupied, busy working on their individual biochemistry projects. She wondered who'd given her the warning and wished she could dismiss the note as a joke, but she couldn't. Especially not after the incident yesterday.

Someone had gotten inside her locker. How the person had known her combination she wasn't sure, since there hadn't been any signs of forced entry. But whoever it was had taken the time to leave things almost exactly as she'd left them.

And now the anonymous note.

Reaching her car, she unlocked the door and got inside, locking it again behind her. After checking her surroundings and the other cars parked close by, she maneuvered out of the parking lot and onto the street. When she came to a stop at the first traffic light, she pulled the typed note from her purse and reread it.

Disappear? How could she do that, even if she wanted to?

She was currently working on her PhD as a biochemist, and was one of five chosen nationally to participate in a yearlong research program at Seton Industries. Crystal knew others were interested in her research. Case in point: just last month she'd been approached by two government officials who wanted her to continue her PhD research under the protection of Homeland Security. The two men had stressed what could happen if her data got into the wrong hands, namely those with criminal intent. She had assured them that even with the documented advances of her research, her project was still just a theoretical concept. But they had wanted to place her in a highly collaborative environment with two other American chemists working on similar research. Although their offer had been tempting, she had turned it down. She was set to graduate from Harvard with her PhD in the spring and had already received a number of job offers.

But now she wondered if she should have taken the men's warning seriously. Could someone with criminal intent be after the findings she'd already logged?

She glanced in her rearview mirror and her heart pounded. A blue car she'd noticed several traffic lights back was still there. Was she imagining things?

A short while later she knew she wasn't. The car was staying a few car lengths behind her.

Crystal knew she couldn't go home. The driver of that blue car would follow her. So where could she go? Who could she call? The four other biochemists were also PhD students, but she stayed to herself the majority of the time and hadn't formed relationships with any of them.

Except for Darnell Enfield. He'd been the one intent on establishing a relationship with her. She had done nothing to encourage the man and had told him countless times she wasn't interested. When that hadn't deterred him, she'd threatened to file a complaint with the director of the program. In anger, Darnell had accused her of being stuck-up, saying he hoped she had a lonely and miserable life.

Crystal had news for him. She had that already. On most days she tried not to dwell on just how lonely the past five years had been. But as far as she was concerned, Loneliness had been her middle name for further back than five years.

Born the only child to older, overprotective parents, she'd been homeschooled and rarely allowed to leave the house except to attend church or accompany them to the grocery store. For years, her parents wouldn't even allow her to go outside and play. She remembered when one of the neighbor kids had tried befriending her, the most she could do was talk to the little girl through her bedroom window.

It was only after their pastor had encouraged her parents to enroll Crystal in public school to enhance her social skills that they did so. By then she was fifteen and starving for friends. But she'd discovered just how cruel the world was when the other girls had snubbed her and the guys had made fun of her because she'd been advanced in all her studies. They'd called her a genius freak. She had been miserable attending school until she'd met Bane.

Brisbane Westmoreland.

The man she had secretly married five years ago on her eighteenth birthday. And the man she hadn't seen since.

As a teenager, Bane had been her best friend, her sounding board and her reason for existing. He'd understood her like no other and she'd felt she had understood him. Her parents made the four-year difference in their ages a big issue and tried keeping them apart. The more her parents tried, the more she'd defied them to be with him.

Then there was the problem of Bane being a Westmoreland. Years ago, her and Bane's great-grandfathers had ended their friendship because of a dispute regarding land boundaries, and it seemed her father had no problem continuing the feud.

When Crystal came to another traffic light she pulled out a business card from her purse. It was the card those two government officials had left with her. They'd asked her to call if she changed her mind or if she noticed any funny business. At the time she'd thought their words were a scare tactic to make her give their offer more consideration. But could they have been right? Should she contact them? She replaced the card in her purse and looked at the note again.

No matter what, don't trust anyone.

So what should she do? Where could she go? Since

her father's death, her mother was now a missionary in Haiti. Should Crystal escape to Orangeburg, South Carolina, where her aunt Rachel still lived? The last thing Crystal wanted was to bring trouble to her elderly aunt's doorstep.

There was another place she could hide. Her childhood home in Denver. She and her mother had discovered, after going through her father's papers, that he'd never sold their family homestead after her parents moved to Connecticut. And even more shocking to Crystal was that he'd left the ranch to her. Had that been his way of letting her know he'd accepted that one day she would go back there?

She nibbled her bottom lip. Should she go back now? And face all the memories she'd left behind? What if Bane was there? What if he'd hooked up with someone else despite the promises he'd made to her?

She didn't want to believe that. The Bane Westmoreland she had fallen in love with had promised to honor their wedding vows. Before marrying someone else he would seek her out to ask for a divorce.

She thought about the other promise he'd made and wondered if she was the biggest fool on earth. He'd vowed he would come back for her. That had been five years ago and she was still waiting. Was she wasting her life on a man who had forgotten about her? A lot could have happened since he'd made that promise. Feelings and emotions could change. People could change. Why was she refusing to let go of teenage memories with a guy who might have moved on with his life?

Legally she was a married woman, but all she had to show for it was a last name she never used and a husband who'd left her with unfulfilled promises. Her last contact with him after her father had sent her away was when he'd called to let her know he was joining the navy. Did he expect her to wait until he got tired of being a sailor, moving from one port to the next? What if an emergency had come up and she'd needed him?

She knew the answer to that without much thought. Had an emergency arisen, she could have reached him through his family. Although the Westmorelands had no idea where she lived now, she'd always known where they were. She could have picked up the phone and called Dillon, Bane's eldest brother, if she'd ever truly wanted or needed to contact Bane. Several times she'd come close to doing that, but something had always held her back. First of all, she knew the Westmorelands blamed her for a lot of the trouble Bane had gotten into.

As teens, her and Bane's relationship had been obsessive and she didn't want to think about the number of times they'd broken the law to be together. She'd had resorted to cutting school, and regardless of what her parents had assumed, the majority of the time it had been her idea and not his. Nothing her parents or his family said or did had torn them apart. Instead, their bond had gotten stronger.

Because of the difference in their ages, her parents had accused Bane of taking advantage of her, and her father had even put a restraining order in place and threatened Bane with jail time to keep him away from her. But that hadn't stopped her or Bane from being together. When they'd gotten tired of their families' interference, they had eloped.

She reached inside her shirt and pulled out the sterling-silver heart-shaped locket Bane had given her instead of a wedding ring he couldn't afford. When he'd placed the locket around her neck he'd said it had belonged to his deceased mother. He'd wanted her to have it, to always wear it as a reminder of their love. His love. She swallowed a thick lump in her throat. If he loved her so much, then why hadn't he kept his promise and come back for her?

Her mother had mentioned that Bane's eldest brother, Dillon, had called a year ago when he'd heard about her father's death. According to her mother, the conversation had been brief, but Dillon had taken the time to inquire about how she was doing. According to her mother the only thing he'd said about Bane was that he was in the navy. Of course her mother thought her daughter was doing just fine now that Bane was out of her life, and the Westmorelands probably felt the same way since she was out of Bane's. What if her mother was right and Bane *was* doing just fine without her?

Drawing in a deep breath, Crystal forced her thoughts back to the car following her. Should she call the police for help? She quickly dismissed the idea. Hadn't the note warned her not to trust anyone? Suddenly an idea popped into her head. It was the start of the holiday shopping season and shoppers were already out in large numbers. She would drive to the busiest mall in Dallas and get lost in traffic. If that didn't work she would come up with plan B.

The one thing she knew for certain was that she would not let the person tail her home. When she got there, she would quickly pack her things and disappear for a while. She would decide where she was going once she got to the airport. The Bahamas sounded pretty good right about now.

What would Seton Industries think when she didn't show up for work as usual? At present that was the least of her worries. Staying safe was her top priority.

Half an hour later she smiled, satisfied that plan A

had worked. All it took was to scoot her car in and out of all those tenacious shoppers a few times, and the driver of the blue car couldn't keep up. But just to be certain, she drove around for a while to make sure she was no longer being tailed.

She had fallen in love with Dallas but had no choice except to leave town for a while.

Sitting in the SUV he had rented at the airport, Bane tilted his Stetson off his eyes and shifted his long legs into a more comfortable position. He checked his watch again. The private investigator's report indicated Crystal was employed with Seton Industries as a biochemist while working on her PhD, and that she usually got off work around four. It was close to seven and she hadn't gotten home yet. So where was she?

It *was* the holiday season and she could have gone shopping. And she must have girlfriends, so she could very well be spending time with one of them. He just had to wait.

None of his family members had been surprised when he'd announced he was going after Crystal. However, except for Bailey, who knew the whole story, all of them were shocked to learn he'd married Crystal when they had eloped. His brother Riley had claimed he'd suspected as much, but all the others hadn't had a clue.

Bailey had given Bane a huge hug and whispered that it was about time he claimed his wife. Of course others, like Dillon, had warned Bane that things might be different and not to expect Crystal to be the eighteen-year-old he'd last seen. Just like he had changed over the years, so had she.

His cousin Zane, who was reputed to be an expert on women, had gone so far as to advise Bane not to expect

Crystal to readily embrace her role as loving wife or his role as long-lost husband. Zane had cautioned him not to do anything stupid like sweeping her off her feet and carrying her straight to the bedroom. They would have to get to know each other all over again, and he shouldn't be surprised if she tried putting up walls between them for a while.

Zane had reiterated that regardless of the reason, Bane hadn't made contact with his wife in almost five years and doubts would have crossed Crystal's mind regarding Bane's love and faithfulness.

He had appreciated everyone's advice. And while he wished like hell he could sweep Crystal off her feet and head straight for the nearest bedroom when he saw her, he had enough sense to know they would have to take things slow. After all, they had been apart all this time and there would be a lot for them to talk about and sort out. But he felt certain she knew he would come back for her as he'd promised; no matter how long it had taken him to do so.

He was back in her life and didn't intend to go anywhere. Even if it meant he lived with her in Dallas for a while. As a SEAL he could live anywhere as long as he was ready to leave for periodic training sessions or covert operations whenever his commanding officer called. And as long as there was still instability in Iraq, Afghanistan and Syria, his team might be needed.

Thinking of his team made him think about Coop. It was hard to believe his friend was gone. All the team members had taken Coop's death hard and agreed that if it was the last thing they did, they would return to Syria, find Coop's body and bring him home. His parents deserved that and Coop did, too.

For the longest time, Bane had thought he could keep

his marriage a secret from his team. But he found it hard to do when the guys thought it was essential that he got laid every once in a while. Things started getting crazy when they tried fixing him up with some woman or another every chance they got.

He'd finally told them about his marriage to Crystal. Then he wished he hadn't when they'd teased him about all the women they were getting while he wasn't getting any. He took it all in stride because he only wanted one woman. His team members accepted that he intended to adhere to his wedding vows and in the end they all respected and admired him for it.

Now the SEAL in him studied his surroundings, taking notice. The one thing he appreciated was that Crystal's home appeared to be in a safe neighborhood. The streets were well lit and the houses spaced with enough distance for privacy yet with her neighbors in reach if needed.

The brick house where she lived suited her. It looked to be in good condition and the yard was well manicured. One thing he did notice was that unlike all the other houses, she didn't have any Christmas decorations. There weren't any colorful lights around her windows or animated objects adorning her lawn. Did she not celebrate the holidays anymore? He recalled a time when she had. In fact the two most important days to her had been her birthday and Christmas.

He'd made her birthday even more special by marrying her on it. A smile touched his lips when he recalled how, over the years, he had bought her birthday cards and anniversary cards, although he hadn't been able to send them to her. He'd even bought her Valentine's Day cards and Christmas cards every year. He had stored them in a trunk, knowing one day he would give them to her. Well, that day had finally arrived and he had all of them packed in his luggage. He had signed each one and taken the time to write a special message inside. Then there were all those letters he'd written. Letters he'd never mailed because he hadn't a clue where to send them.

He'd made Bailey promise not to tell him because if he'd known how to get to Crystal he would have gone to her and messed up all the effort he'd made in becoming the type of man who could give her what she deserved in life.

Five years was a long time and there had been times he'd thought he would lose his mind from missing her so much. It had taken all he had, every bit of resolve he could muster, to make it through. In the end, he knew the sacrifice would be worth it.

He figured he would give Crystal time to get into the house before he got out of the car and knocked on the door, so as not to spook her. No need to give her neighbors anything to talk about, either, especially if no one knew she was married. And from the private investigator's report, her marital status was a guarded secret. He understood and figured it wouldn't be easy to explain a husband who'd gone AWOL.

His phone rang and a smile tugged at the corner of his mouth when he recognized the ringtone. It was Thurston McRoy, better known to the team as Mac. All Bane's team members' names had been shortened for easy identification during deployment. Cooper was Coop. McRoy was Mac. And because his name was Brisbane, the nickname his family had given him was already a shortened version, so his team members called him Bane like everyone else.

"What's up, Mac?"

"Have you seen her yet?"

He had spoken to Mac on his way to the airport to let him know his whereabouts, just in case the team was needed somewhere. "No, not yet. I'm parked outside her place. She's late getting off work."

"When she gets there, don't ask a lot of questions and please don't go off on her as if you've been there for the past five years. You may think she's late but it might be her usual MO to get delayed every once in a while. Women do have days they like to get prettied up. Get their hair and nails done and stuff."

Bane chuckled. He figured Mac would know since he was one of the married team members. And Mac would tell them that after every extended mission, he would go home to an adjustment period, where he would have to get to know his wife all over again and reclaim his position as head of the house.

When Bane saw car lights headed toward where he was parked, he said, "I think this is her pulling up now."

"Great. Just remember the advice I gave you."

Yours and everybody else's, Bane thought. "Whatever. I know how to handle my business."

"See that you do." Then without saying anything else, Mac clicked off the phone.

As Bane watched the headlights get closer, he couldn't stop the deep pounding of his heart. He wondered what changes to expect. Did Crystal wear her hair down to her shoulders like she had years ago? Did she nibble her bottom lip when she was nervous about something? And did she still have those sexy legs?

It didn't matter. He intended to finally claim her as his. His wife.

Bane watched as she pulled into her yard and got out of the car. The moment his gaze latched on to her all the emotion he hadn't been able to contain over the years washed over him, putting an ache in his gut.

The streetlight shone on her features. Even from the distance, he could see she was beautiful. She'd grown taller and her youthful figure had blossomed into that of a woman. His pulse raced as he studied how well her curves filled out her dark slacks and how her breasts appeared to be shaped perfectly beneath her jacket.

As he watched her, the navy SEAL in him went on alert. Something wasn't right. He had been trained to be vigilant not just to his surroundings but also to people. Recognizing signs of trouble had kept him alive on more than one mission. Maybe it was the quickness of her steps to her front door, the number of times she looked back over her shoulder or the way she kept checking the street as if to make certain she hadn't been followed.

When she went inside and closed the door he released the breath he only realized now that he'd been holding. Who or what had her so antsy? She had no knowledge that he was coming, so it couldn't be him. She seemed more than just rattled. Terrified was more like it. Why? Even if she'd somehow found out he was coming, she had no reason of be afraid of him. Unless...

He scowled. What if she assumed he wasn't coming back for her and she'd taken a lover? What if she was the mother of another man's child? What if...

He cleared his mind. Each of those thoughts was like a quick punch to his gut, and he refused to go there. Besides, the private investigator's report had been clear. She lived alone and was not involved with anyone.

Still, something had her frightened.

After waiting for several minutes to give her time to

get settled after a day at work, he opened the door to the SUV. It was time to find out what the hell was going on.

With her heart thundering hard in her chest, Crystal began throwing items in the suitcase open on her bed. Had she imagined it or had she been watched when she'd entered her home tonight? She had glanced around several times and hadn't noticed anything or anyone. But still…

She took a deep breath, knowing she couldn't lose her cool. She had to keep a level head. She made a decision to leave her car here and a few lights burning inside her house to give the impression she was home. She would call a cab to take her to the airport and would take only the necessities and a few items of clothing. She could buy anything else she needed.

But this, she thought, studying the photo album she held in her hand, went everywhere with her. She had purchased it right after her last phone call with Bane. Her parents had sent Crystal to live with Aunt Rachel to finish out the last year of school. They'd wanted to get her away from Bane, not knowing she and Bane had married.

Before they'd returned home after eloping, Bane had convinced Crystal it was important for her to finish school before telling anyone they'd gotten married. He'd told her that if her parents tried keeping them apart that he would put up with it for a few months, which was the time it would take for her to finish school. They hadn't counted on her parents sending her away. But still, she believed that Bane would come for her once the school year ended, no matter where she was.

But a couple of months after she left Denver, she'd gotten a call from him. She'd assumed he was calling to let her know he couldn't stand the separation and was coming for her. But his real purpose had been twofold. He'd wanted to find out if she had gotten pregnant when they eloped, and he'd told her he'd enlisted in the navy and would be leaving for boot camp in Great Lakes, Illinois, in a few weeks. He'd said he needed to grow up, become responsible and make something out of himself. She deserved a man who could be all that he could be, and after he'd accomplished that goal he would come for her. He'd also promised that while they were apart he would honor their wedding vows and she'd promised him the same. And she had.

She'd figured he would be in the navy for four years. Preparing for the separation, she'd decided to make something of herself, as well. He deserved that, too. So after completing high school she'd enrolled in college. She had taken a placement test, which she'd aced. Instead of being accepted as a freshman, she had entered as a junior.

Sitting on the edge of the bed now, she flipped through the album, which she had dedicated to Bane. She'd even had his name engraved on the front. While they were apart she'd kept this photo journal, chronicling her life without him. There were graduation pictures from high school and college, random pictures she'd taken just for him. She'd figured that by the time she saw him she would have at least two to three years' worth of photos. She hadn't counted on the bulky album containing five years of photographs. The last thing she'd assumed was that they would be apart for this long without any contact.

She thought of him often. Every day. What she tried not to think about was why it was taking him so long to come back for her, or how he might be somewhere en-

joying life without her. Forcing those thoughts from her
mind, she packed the album in her luggage. Her destination was the Bahamas. She had done an online bank
transfer to her "fun" account, which had accumulated
a nice amount due to the vacations she'd never gotten
around to taking. And in case her home was searched,
she'd made sure not to leave any clues about where she
was headed.

Was she being impulsive by heeding what the note
had said when she didn't even know who'd written it?
She could report it, what happened to her locker and
that she'd noticed someone following her to those two
government officials. If she couldn't trust her own government, then who could she trust? She shook her head,
deciding against making that call. Maybe she'd watched
too many TV shows where the government had turned
out to be the bad guy.

Crystal thought about calling her mother and Aunt
Rachel, and then decided against it. Whatever she was
involved with, it would be best to leave them out of it.
She would contact them later when she felt doing so
would be safe. Moments later, she had rolled her luggage out of her bedroom into the living room and was
calling for a cab when her doorbell rang.

She went still. Nobody ever visited her. Who would
be doing so now? She crept back into the shadows of
her hallway, hoping whoever was at the door would
think she wasn't home. She held her breath when the
doorbell sounded again. Had the person on the other
side seen her enter her house and knew she was there?

Moments passed and the doorbell did not sound
again. She sighed in relief—and then there was a hard
knock. She swallowed. The person hadn't gone away.
Either she answered it or continued to pretend she

wasn't there. Since the latter hadn't worked so far, she rushed into her bedroom and grabbed her revolver out of the nightstand drawer.

She'd grown up around guns, and thanks to Bane she knew how to use one. This neighborhood was pretty safe, and even though she'd figured she'd never need to use it, she had bought the gun anyway. A woman living alone needed to be cautious.

By the time she'd made it back to the living room, there was a second knock. She moved toward the door, but stopped five feet away. She called out, "Who is it?" and tightened her hands on the revolver.

There was a moment of silence. And then a voice said, "It's me, Crystal. Bane."

Two

The revolver Crystal held almost fell from her hand.

Bane? My Bane? No way, she thought, backing up. It had to be an impostor. It didn't even sound like Bane. This voice was deeper, huskier.

If it was a trick, who knew of her relationship with Brisbane Westmoreland? And if it really was Bane, why had he shown up on her doorstep now? Why tonight of all nights?

It just wasn't logical for her to have been thinking about him only moments ago and for him to be here now. She would go with her first assumption. The person at the door claiming to be Bane wasn't him.

"You aren't Bane. Go away or I'll call the police," she threatened loudly. "I have a gun and will shoot if I have to."

"Crystal Gayle, it *is* me. Honest. It's Bane."

Crystal Gayle? She sucked in a deep breath. Nobody

called her that but her parents…and Bane. When she was young, she had hated being called by her first and middle names, which her father had given her, naming her after his favorite country singer. But Bane had made her like it when he'd called her that on occasion. Could it really be him at the door?

Lowering the gun, she looked out the peephole. Her gaze connected to a gorgeous pair of hazel eyes with a greenish tint. They were eyes she knew. It *was* Bane.

She was about to open the door when she remembered the note. *Trust no one*. But this wasn't just anyone, she reasoned with herself. This was Bane.

She unlocked the door and stepped back. Soft porch light poured into her foyer as Bane eased open the door. He'd always been tall and lanky, but the man entering her house appeared a lot taller than she remembered. And he was no longer slender. He was all muscles and they were in perfect proportion to his height and weight. It was obvious he worked out a lot to stay in shape. His body exemplified endurance and strength. And when her gaze settled on his face, she drew in a deep, sharp breath. He even looked different. Rougher. Tougher.

The eyes were the same but she'd never seen him with facial hair before. He'd always been handsome in a boyish sort of way, but his features now were perfectly masculine. They appeared chiseled, his lips sculpted. She was looking into the most handsome face she'd ever seen.

He not only looked older and more mature, but he also looked military—even while wearing jeans, a chambray shirt, a leather bomber jacket, Western boots and a Stetson. There was something about the way he stood, upright and straight. And all this transformation had come from being in the navy?

He closed the door behind him, staring at her just as she was staring at him. Her heart pounded. A part of her wanted to race over to him, tell him how glad she was to see him, how much she had missed him…but she couldn't. Her legs refused to move and she knew why. This Bane was like a stranger to her.

"Crystal."

She hadn't imagined it. His voice had gotten deeper. Sounded purely sexy to her ears. "Bane."

"You look good."

She blinked at his words and said the first thing that came to her mind. "You look good, too. And different."

He smiled and her breath caught. He still had that Brisbane Westmoreland smile. The one that spread across a full mouth and showed teeth that were perfectly even and sparkling white against mocha-colored skin. The familiarity warmed her inside.

"I am different. I'm not the same Bane. The military has a way of doing that to you," he said, in that husky voice she was trying to get used to hearing.

He was admitting to being different.

Was this his way of saying his transformation had changed his preferences? Like his taste in women? He was older now, five years older, in fact. Had he shown up on her doorstep tonight of all nights to let her know that he wanted a divorce?

Fine, she would deal with it. She had no choice. Besides, she wasn't sure if she would like the new Bane anyway. He was probably doing her a favor.

"Okay," she said, placing her revolver on the coffee table. "If you brought any papers with you that require my signature, then give them to me."

He lifted a brow. "Papers?"

"Yes."

"What kind of papers?"

Instead of answering, she glanced at her watch. She needed to call a cab to the airport. The plane to the Bahamas would take off in three hours.

"Crystal? What kind of papers are you talking about?"

She glanced back over at him. And why did her gaze automatically go to his mouth, the same mouth that had taught her how to kiss and given her so much pleasure? And why was she recalling a lot of those kisses right now? She drew in a deep, shallow breath. "Divorce papers."

"Is that why you think I'm here?"

Was she imagining things or had his voice sounded brisk? She shrugged. Why were they even having this conversation? Why couldn't he just give her the papers and be on his way so she could be on hers? After all, it had been five years. She got that. Did it matter that she had spent all that time waiting for him to show up?

"Crystal? Is that why you think I'm here? To ask for a divorce?" He repeated the question and she noticed his tone still had a brusque edge.

She held his gaze. "What other reason could there be?"

He shoved his hands into the pockets of his jeans and braced his legs apart in a stance that was as daunting as it was sexy. It definitely brought emphasis to his massive shoulders, the solidness of chest and his chiseled good looks.

"Did you consider that maybe I'm here to keep that promise I made about coming back for you?"

She blinked, not sure she'd heard him correctly. "You aren't here to ask for a divorce?"

"No. What makes you think I'd want to divorce you?"

She could give him a number of reasons once her

head stopped spinning. Instead, she said what was in the forefront of her mind. "Well, it has been five years, Bane."

"I told you I'd come back for you."

She placed her hands on her hips. "Yes, but I hadn't counted on it being *five* years. Five years without a single word from you. Besides, you just said you've changed."

The look in his eyes indicated he was having a hard time keeping up with her. "I *have* changed, Crystal. Being a SEAL has a way of changing you, but that has nothing to do—"

"SEAL? You're a navy SEAL?"

"Yes."

Now she was the one having a hard time keeping up. "I knew you'd joined the navy, but I figured you'd been assigned to a ship somewhere."

He nodded. "I would have been if my captain in boot camp hadn't thought I would be a good fit for the SEALs. He cut through a lot of red tape for me to go to the naval academy."

That was another surprise. "You attended the naval academy?"

"Yes."

Jeez. She was realizing just how little she knew about what he'd been doing over the past five years. "I didn't know."

He shifted his stance and her gaze followed the movement, taking in his long, denim-clad, boot-wearing legs.

"Bailey said the two of you lost contact with each other a couple of years ago," he said.

Now was the time to come clean and say losing contact with Bailey had been a deliberate move. The periodic calls from his cousin had become depressing since they'd agreed Crystal wouldn't ask about Bane. Just as he wouldn't ask Bailey any questions about Crystal.

That had been Bane's idea. He'd figured the less they knew about the other's lives, the less chance they had of reneging on their promise not to seek the other out before he could meet his goals.

During one of those conversations Bailey had informed her Bane had set up a bank account for her, in case she ever needed anything. She never had and to this day she'd never withdrawn any funds.

"Even if Bailey and I had kept in touch, she would not have told me *what* you were doing, just *how* you were doing. That was the agreement, remember, Bane?"

"You could have called Dil," he said as he raked his gaze over her.

He was probably taking note of how she'd changed as she'd done with him. He could clearly see she was no longer the eighteen-year-old he'd married, but was now a twenty-three-year-old woman. Her birthday had been two weeks ago. She wondered if he'd remembered.

"No, I couldn't call your brother, or any other member of your family for that matter, and you know why. They blamed me for you getting into trouble."

Crystal glanced at her watch again. He'd said he was here to fulfill his promise. If he was doing it because he felt obligated then she would release him from it. Although asking for a divorce might not have been his original intent, she was certain it was crossing his mind now. Why wouldn't it? They were acting like strangers instead of two people who'd once been so obsessed with each other they'd eloped. Why weren't they all over each other? Why was he over there and she still standing over here? The answer to both questions was so brutally clear she had to force tears from her eyes.

Like he said, he had changed. He was a SEAL. Something other than her was number one in his life now. More than likely it had been his missions that had kept him away all this time. He'd chosen what he really wanted.

"Crystal, I have a question for you."

His words interrupted her thoughts. "What?"

"Why did you come to the door with a gun?"

It had taken every ounce of Bane's control not to cross the room and pull his wife into his arms. How often had he dreamed of this moment, wished for it, yearned for it? But things weren't playing out like he'd hoped.

Although he'd taken heed to Zane's warning and not swept her off her feet and headed for the nearest bedroom, he hadn't counted on not getting at least a kiss, a hug…something. But she stood there as if she wasn't sure what to make of his appearance here tonight. And he still couldn't grasp why she assumed he wanted a divorce just because he'd told her he'd changed. He'd changed for the better, not only for himself but also for her. Now he had something to offer her. He could give her the life she deserved.

Crystal nibbled her bottom lip, which had always been an indication she was nervous about something. Damn, she looked good. Time had only enhanced her beauty, and where in the hell had all those curves come from?

She had changed into a pair of skinny jeans, a pullover sweater and boots. She looked all soft and feminine. So gorgeous. Her hair was not as long as it used to be. Instead of flowing past her shoulders it barely touched them. The new style suited her. How had she managed to keep the guys away? He was certain that with her beauty there had been a number of men who'd come around over the years.

Even now Bane's hands itched to touch her all over like he used to. He would give anything to run his fingers across the curve of her hips and buttocks and cup her breasts.

"The gun?"

Her question pulled his concentration back to their conversation. Probably for the best, since the thought of what he wanted to do with his hands was turning him on big-time. "Yes. I watched you get out of your car to come into the house and you seemed nervous. Is something going on? Is some man harassing you or stalking you?"

She lifted a brow. "A man stalking me? What makes you think that?"

He held her gaze. "I told you. I noticed you were nervous and—"

"Yes, I got that part," she interrupted to say. "But what makes you think any man would stalk me?"

Had she looked in the mirror lately? If she'd asked him *why* he thought she was being stalked, then he could have told her that his SEAL training had taught him how to zero in on certain things. But her question had been what made him think *any man* would want to stalk *her*. That was a different question altogether. He could see a man becoming obsessed with her. Hadn't Bane?

"You're a very beautiful woman. You've always been beautiful, Crystal. You're even more so now."

She shook her head. "Beautiful? You're laying it on thick, aren't you, Bane?"

"No, I don't think so. Level with me. Is there some man stalking you? Is that why you had the gun? And what's with the luggage? You're going someplace?"

She broke eye contact with him to shrug. "The gun is to protect myself."

Bane had a feeling that wasn't all there was to it. When he'd first walked into her house he'd seen the luggage, but his mind had been solely on her, entranced with her beauty. This older version of Crystal sent his heart pounding into overdrive. It had been a long time. Too long.

He turned his concentration back to what she'd just told him. "You have the gun to protect yourself... I can buy that, although this seems to be a pretty safe neighborhood," he said. "But that doesn't explain why you were ready to shoot. Has your home been broken into before?"

"No."

"Then what's going on?"

Even after all this time he still could read her like a book. She had a tendency to lick her lips when she was nervous, and unconsciously shift her body from side to side while standing on the balls of her feet. He could tell she was trying to decide how to answer his question. That didn't sit well with him. In the past, he and Crystal never kept secrets from each other. So why was she doing so now?

"After all this time, you don't have the right to ask me anything, Bane."

You're wrong about that, sweetheart.

Without thinking about what he was doing, he closed the distance separating them to stand directly in front of her. "I believe I do have that right. As long as we're still legally married, Crystal, I have every right."

She lifted her chin and pinched her lips together. "Fine. Then, we can get a divorce."

"Not happening." He rubbed his hand down his face. What the hell was going on here? Not only was this reunion not going the way he'd wanted, it had just taken a bad turn.

He looked at her, somewhat bewildered by her refusal to answer his question. "I'm asking again, Crystal. What's going on with you? Why the gun and the packed luggage?"

When she didn't answer, standing there with a mutinous expression on her face, he then asked the one question he hadn't wanted to ask, but needed to know. And he hoped like hell he was wrong.

"Are you involved with someone who's causing you problems?"

Three

That question set Crystal off. She took the final step to completely close the distance between them. "Involved with someone? Are you accusing me of being unfaithful?"

"Not accusing you of anything," he said in a tone that let her know her outrage had fueled his. "But I find it odd you won't answer my question. Why are you acting so secretive? You've never acted that way with me before."

No, she hadn't. But then the Bane she used to know, the one she'd loved more than life itself, would not have forgotten her for five years. He would have moved heaven, hell and any place in between to have her with him so the two of them could be together.

"You're not the only one who's changed. Just like you're not the same, I'm not the same."

They faced off. She didn't see him move, but suddenly his body brushed against hers and she drew in a sharp breath. The touch had been electric, sending a sizzle through her. Suddenly, her mind was filled with memories of the last time they'd touched. Really touched. All over. Naked. Those memories were enough to ignite a fire in the pit of her stomach.

"You may not be the same," he said, breaking into the silence between them, speaking in a low tone, "but you kept your wedding vows."

He spoke with such absolute certainty, she wondered how he could be so sure. But of course he was right. "Yes, I kept them."

He nodded. "And before doubt starts clouding that pretty little head of yours, let me go on record to say that I might not be the same, but I kept my wedding vows, as well."

There was no way. Not that she didn't think he would have tried, but she knew when it came to sex, some men classified it as a *must have*. She of all people knew how much the old Bane had enjoyed it. There was no reason to think the new and different Bane wouldn't like it just as much. Just look at him. He was more masculine, more virile—so macho. Even if he hadn't targeted women, they would definitely have targeted him.

"Now that we have that cleared up…"

Did they? "Not so fast," she said, trying to ignore it when his body brushed against hers again. Had it been intentional? And why hadn't one of them taken a step back? "What kept you sane?"

"Sane?"

"Yes. You know. From climbing the walls and stuff. I heard men need sex every so often."

He smiled and the force of it sent her senses reeling. "Remind me to give you all the details one day. Now, back to our earlier topic, why did you come to the door with a gun and why the packed bags?"

They were back to that?

But then maybe they should be. She needed to call a cab and get to the airport. And just like she didn't want to involve her mother and Aunt Rachel in whatever was going on, she definitely didn't want to involve Bane. Maybe she should have lied and said she was involved with someone else. Then he would have gotten angry and left, and she would be free to do as the note advised and disappear. Whatever was going on was her issue and not his.

She nibbled her lips as she tried coming up with something that would sound reasonable. Something that wasn't too much of a lie. So she said, "The reason for the packed luggage is because I'm taking a trip."

He looked at her as if to say *duh*. Instead, he held her gaze and asked, "Business or pleasure?"

"Business."

"Where are you headed?"

If she told him the Bahamas, he would question if it really was a business trip, so she said, "Chicago."

"Fine. I'll go with you."

She blinked, suddenly feeling anxiety closing in on her. "Go with me?"

"Yes. I'm on leave so I can do that," he said calmly. "Besides, it's time I got to know you again, and I want you to get to know me."

She drew in a breath, feeling her control deteriorating. Those hazel eyes had always been her weakness.

She knew she was a goner when he asked in a husky voice, "You do want to get to know me all over again, don't you, Crystal Gayle?"

Getting to know Brisbane Westmoreland the first

time around had been like a roller coaster, and she'd definitely enjoyed the ride. There was no doubt that getting to know the new Bane would be even more exhilarating. Now she could enjoy the ride as a woman in control of her own destiny and not as a girl whose life was dictated by her parents. A woman who was older, mature and could appreciate the explosiveness of a relationship with him.

As if he knew what she was thinking and wanted to drive that point home, he caressed the side of her face with the tip of his finger. "I definitely want to get to know you again, Crystal."

Then he brought her body closer to his. She felt his erection pressing hard against her middle and a craving she'd tried to put to rest years ago reared its greedy head, making her force back a moan. When his finger left her face to tug on a section of her hair, sensations she hadn't felt in years ran rampant through her womb.

She stared into his eyes. Hazel eyes that had literally branded her the first time she'd gazed into them. Eyes belonging to Bane. *Her* Bane. And he had admitted just moments ago to keeping their vows all this time. That meant he had five years of need and hunger stored inside him. The thought sent heated blood racing through her veins.

Then he shifted. The movement nudged his knees between hers so she could feel his hard bulge even more. Intentional or not, she wasn't sure. The only thing she was certain about was that if she didn't get her self-control back, she would jump his bones without a second thought. And that wasn't good. She didn't even know him anymore.

He leaned in slowly—too slowly, which let her know this side of Bane wasn't different...at least when it came to this. He'd always let her establish the pace, so as not to take advantage of the difference in their ages and experience levels. She'd always known she hadn't been Bane's first girl, but he'd been her first guy. And he'd always handled her with tenderness.

Bane was letting her take the lead now, and she intended to take it to a whole other level. At that moment, she didn't care that they'd both changed; she wanted his hands on her and his tongue in her mouth. To be totally honest, she needed more but she would settle for those two things now…even if she knew there probably wouldn't be a later.

He bent his head closer, and she refused to consider anything other than what she wanted, needed and had gone five years without. She clutched tight to his shoulders and leaned up on tiptoes to cover his mouth with hers.

Bane wasn't sure what was more dangerous. Storming an extremist stronghold in the middle of the night, or having his way with Crystal's mouth after all these years of going without her taste. But now was not the time to dwell on it. It was time to act.

The way their mouths mated seemed as natural as breathing, and he was glad time had not diminished the desire they'd always shared.

When she slid her tongue inside his mouth, memories of the last time they'd kissed flooded his mind. It had been on their wedding day, during their honeymoon in a small hotel in Utah. He recalled very little about the room itself, only what they'd done within those four walls. And they'd done plenty.

But now, this very minute, they were making new memories. He had dreamed about, thought about and wished for this moment for so long. She took the kiss deeper and he wrapped his arms around her waist and pulled her closer, loving the feel of her body plastered against his.

He loved her taste. Always had and always would. When she sucked on his tongue, his heartbeat thundered in his chest and his erection throbbed mercilessly behind his zipper. He was tempted to devour her and tried like hell to keep his self-control in check. But it became too much. Five years without her had taken its toll.

Suddenly he became the aggressor, taking her mouth with a hunger he felt all the way to the soles of his feet. He wanted her to feel him in every part of her body. And when he finally caught her wriggling tongue, he feasted on it.

The one thing that had consumed his mind on their wedding day was the same thing consuming his mind right now. Crystal was his. Undeniably, unquestionably and indisputably his.

He thrust his tongue even deeper into her mouth. He knew he had to pull back; otherwise he would consume her whole. Especially now, when he was filled with the need to do the one thing he shouldn't do, which was to sweep her off her feet and head for the nearest bedroom. He had wanted this moment for so long… Kissing her filled him with sensations so deliciously intoxicating that he could barely think straight.

Bane knew he was embarking on a mission more dangerous than any he'd gone on as a SEAL. Crystal had always been both his weakness and his strength. She was an ache he'd always had to ease. Some way, somehow, he had to show her, prove to her, that any changes he'd made over the past five years were all good and would benefit both of them. Otherwise, the time they'd spent apart would have been for nothing. He refused to accept that.

Reluctant to do so but knowing he should, Bane ended the kiss. But he wasn't ready to release her yet and his hands moved from her waist to boldly cup her backside. And while she was snuggled so close to him, his hands moved up and down the length of her spine before returning to cup her backside again. Now that she was back in his life, he couldn't imagine her being out of it again.

That thought drove him to reiterate something he'd said earlier. "I'm going to Chicago with you."

Slowly recovering from their kiss, Crystal tilted her head back and gazed up at Bane. Her lips had ground against his. Her tongue had initiated a dance inside his mouth that had been as perfect as anything she'd ever known. And he had reciprocated by kissing her back with equal need. Waves of passion had consumed her, nearly drowning her.

But now she had reclaimed her senses and the words he'd spoken infiltrated her mind. She knew there was no way he could go anywhere with her. She was about to open her mouth to tell him so when her cell phone rang. She tensed. Who could be contacting her? She seldom got calls.

"You plan on getting that?" Bane murmured the question while placing a kiss on the side of her neck.

She swallowed. Should she? It could be the airline calling her for some reason. She had left them her number in case her flight was delayed or canceled. "Yes," she said, quickly moving away from him to grab the phone off the table, right next to where she had laid the gun. Seeing the weapon was a reminder of what she had to do and why she couldn't let Bane sidetrack her.

She clicked on her cell phone. "Hello?"

"Don't try getting away, Ms. Newsome. We will find you." And then she heard a click ending the call.

Crystal's heart thumped painfully in her chest. Who was the caller? How did the person get her private number? How did the person know she was trying to get away? She turned toward Bane. Something in her eyes must have told him the call had troubled her because he quickly crossed the room to her. "Crystal, what's wrong?"

She took a deep breath, not knowing what to do or say. She stared up at him as she nervously bit her lip. Should she level with Bane and tell him everything that was going on? The note had said not to trust anyone, but how could she not trust the one and only person she'd always trusted?

"I don't know what's wrong," she said quietly.

She pulled away to reach for her purse and retrieve the note. "I got this note at work today," she said, handing it to him. "And I don't know who sent it."

She waited while he read it and when he glanced back up at her, she said, "Yesterday someone broke into my locker at work, and I noticed someone following me home today."

"Following you?"

"Yes. I thought maybe I was imagining things at first, but when the driver stayed discreetly behind me, I knew that I wasn't. I deliberately lost the car in all the holiday shoppers at one of the busiest malls."

"What about that phone call just now?" he asked, studying her.

She told him what the caller had said. "I don't know who it was or how they got my number."

Bane didn't say anything for a minute. "Is that the reason for the packed bags? You're doing what the note said and disappearing?"

"Yes. Those guys said craziness might start happening and—"

Bane frowned. "What guys?"

"Last month while I was eating lunch at a restaurant near work, I was approached by two government men. They showed me credentials to prove it. They knew about the project I'm working on at Seton and said Homeland Security was concerned about my research getting into the wrong hands. They offered me a chance to work for the government at some lab in DC, along with two other chemists who're working on similar research."

"And?"

"I turned them down. They accepted my answer, but warned me that there were people out there with criminal intent who would do just about anything to get their hands on my research. They gave me their business card and told me to call them if any craziness happened."

"Have you called them?"

"No. After reading the note I wasn't sure who I could trust. At this point that includes Homeland Security."

"Do you still have the business card those guys gave you?"

"Yes."

"May I see it?"

"Yes." She reached for her purse again. She handed the card to him and watched him study it before snapping several pictures of it with his mobile phone.

"What are you doing?"

He glanced over at her. "Verifying those guys are who they say they are. I'm sending this to someone who can do that for me." He then handed her back the card. "Just what kind of research are you working on?"

She paused a moment before saying. "Obscured Reality, or OR as it's most often called."

"Obscured Reality?"

She nodded. "Yes. It's the ability to make objects invisible."

Four

Bane lifted a brow. "Did you say your research was finding a way to make objects invisible?"

"Yes. Although it hasn't been perfected yet, it won't be long before I perform the first test."

Because he was a SEAL, Bane was aware of advances in technology that most people didn't know about, especially when it came to advanced weapons technology. But he'd never considered that objects could become invisible to the naked eye. He could imagine the chaos it would cause if such a thing fell into the wrong hands.

"And you think this note is legit?" he asked.

"If I doubted it before, that phone call pretty much proved otherwise. That's why I'm leaving."

He nodded. "And that's why I'm going with you."

She shook her head. "You can't go with me, Bane, and I don't have time to argue with you about it. I need to get to the airport."

Argue?

It suddenly dawned on him that in all the years he and Crystal had been together, mostly sneaking around to do so, they'd never argued. They had always been of one accord, always in sync with their thoughts, plans and ideas. The very concept of them not agreeing about something just couldn't compute with him. Of course it would be logical not to be in complete harmony since they were different people now.

Even so, him going with her was not up for discussion.

"How were you planning to get to the airport? Drive?" he asked her.

She shook her head. "No. I was going to call a cab and leave my car here."

"Then, I will take you. We can talk some more on the way."

"Okay, let me close up everything. Won't take but a second."

His gaze followed her movements as she went from room to room turning off lights and unplugging electrical items. Her movements were swift, yet sexy as hell and his body responded to them. She'd always had a cute shape, but this grown-up Crystal was rocking curves like he couldn't believe.

Earlier she had asked how he'd maintained his sanity without sex. He wondered how she'd maintained hers. They had enjoyed each other and he was convinced the only reason she hadn't gotten pregnant was because when it came to her, he'd always been responsible. A teenage pregnancy was something neither of them had needed to deal with.

She leaned down to pick up something off the floor and the way the denim stretched across her shapely

backside sent heat rushing through him. He drew in a
deep breath. Now was not the time to think about how
hot his wife was. What should be consuming his mind
was finding out the identity of the person responsible
for her fleeing her home. Whoever was messing with
her would definitely have to deal with him.

"At least I'm going where there's plenty of sunshine."

His brow furrowed. Did she honestly think there was
sunshine in Chicago this time of the year? She met his
gaze and he knew from the uh-oh look on her face that
she'd unintentionally let that slip.

He was reminded now that although they'd never
argued, they had lied quite a few times. But never to
each other. Mainly the fibs had been for their families.
They'd gotten good at it, although Dillon would catch
Bane in his lies more often than not.

Crossing the room, Bane stopped in front of her.
"You lied to me about where you're going, didn't you?"

She took a deep breath and he could hear the beats
of her heart. They were coming fast and furious. Bane
wasn't sure whether her heart was pounding because he
was confronting her about the lie or because his near-
ness unnerved her like hers did him. Even when he
should be upset about her lying to him, all he wanted
to do was lean in closer and taste her again.

"Yes, I lied. I'm not going to Chicago but to the Bahamas. But when I lied about it, it was for your own
good."

"For my own good?" he repeated as if making sure
he'd heard her right.

"Yes. In the past I was the reason you got into trouble. Now you're a SEAL and I won't be responsible for
you getting into more trouble on my account."

He stared at her. Didn't she know whatever he'd done

in the past had been of his own free will? During those days he would have done anything to be with her. There was no way he could have stayed away as her father had demanded. Her parents hadn't even given them a chance just because Bane's last name was Westmoreland. Although Carl Newsome had claimed Bane's age had been the major factor, Bane often wondered if that was true.

Everyone knew how much he'd loved Crystal. Members of his family had thought he was insane, and in a way he had been. Insanely in love. Hadn't his brother Riley even told him once that no man should love any female that much? Bane wondered if Riley was singing that same tune now that he was married to Alpha. Bane doubted it. All it took was to see his brother and Alpha together to know Riley now understood how deeply a man could love a woman.

"Crystal?" he said, trying to keep his voice on a serious note because he knew she actually believed what she'd said. "Stop thinking you're the reason I was such a badass back in the day. When I met you I was already getting into trouble with the law. After I hooked up with you, I actually got in less trouble."

She rolled her eyes. "That's not the way I remember it."

"You remember it the way your parents wanted you to remember it. Yes, I deliberately defied your father whenever he tried keeping us apart, but it wasn't as if I was a gangster or anything."

A smile curved his lips as he continued, "At least not after meeting you. With you I was on my best behavior. You even nailed the reason I behaved that way. You're the one who pointed out it had everything to do with the loss of my parents and aunt and uncle in that plane crash. The depth of our grief overpowered me, Bailey and the twins, and getting into trouble was our outlet. That just goes to show how smart you were even back then, and your theory made sense. Remember all those long talks we used to have?"

She nodded. "Yes, by the side of the road or in our private place. Our family thought all those times the sheriff found us that we were making out in your truck or something. And all we'd been doing was talking. I tried telling my parents that but they wouldn't listen. You were a Westmoreland and they wanted to think the worst. They believed I was sexually active when I wasn't."

He recalled those times. Yes, they had been caught parking, and cutting school had become almost the norm, but all they'd done was spend time together talking. He'd refused to go all the way with her until she was older. The first time they'd had sex was when she'd turned seventeen. By then they'd been together almost two years.

At least Dillon had believed Bane when he'd told his brother he hadn't touched her. However, given their relationship, it would have been crazy to think they wouldn't get around to making love one day, and Dillon had had the common sense to know that. Instead of giving Bane grief about it, his older brother had lectured him about being responsible and taking precautions.

Bane would never forget the night they'd finally made love. And it hadn't been in the backseat of his truck. He had taken her to the cabin he'd built as a gift for her seventeenth birthday. He'd constructed it on the land he was to inherit, Bane's Ponderosa.

It was a night he would never forget. Waiting had almost done them in, but in the end they'd known they'd done the right thing. That night had been so unbeliev-

ably special and he'd known she would be his forever.
He knew on that night that one day he would make her
his wife.

In fact it had been that night when he'd asked her to
marry him once she finished school, and she'd agreed.
And that had been the plan until her parents made things
even worse for them after she'd turned seventeen.

Crystal had retaliated by refusing to go to school.
And when her parents had threatened to have him put
in jail if he came on their property, he and Crystal had
eloped. He hadn't counted on her parents sending her
away the moment Sheriff Harper found them.

Bane had come close to telling everyone they'd gotten married; no one had the right to separate them. But
something Dillon had said about the future had given
him pause.

Once he'd revealed they were married, he'd known
Crystal would not go back to school. And he of all people had known just how smart she was.

That was when he'd decided to make the sacrifice
and let her go. That had been the hardest decision he'd
ever made. Lucky for him, Bailey had put her pickpock-
eting skills to work and swiped old man Newsome's cell
phone to get Crystal's aunt's phone number.

"I need to go, Bane," Crystal said, intruding into his
memories. "I'll give you my number and we can talk
when I get to where I'm going."

Then in a rush, she added, "I'll call to let you know
when I arrive in the Bahamas so you'll know I'm okay."

He stared at her. Evidently she didn't get it and it was
about time that she did. "Crystal," he said in what he
hoped was a tone that grabbed her absolute attention.
When she stared at him he knew it had. "If you think
I'm going to let you disappear on your own, then you

really don't know me. The old Bane did let you disappear when your father sent you away. But at the time I figured it was for your own good. But those days are over. There's no way in hell you're disappearing on me again."

From her blistering scowl he could tell she didn't appreciate what he'd said. When she opened her mouth to reply, he quickly held up his hand. "I know it's been five years and that we have changed. But there's something with us that hasn't changed."

"What?" she asked in an annoyed tone.

"No matter what happens, we're in this together. That's how things have always been with us, right?"

"Yes, but that was then, Bane."

"And that's how it is now. We're married," he said, touching the locket he'd given her on their wedding day. Just knowing she was still wearing it meant everything to him. "We're in this together, Crystal. Got that?"

For a minute Crystal didn't say anything and then through clenched teeth, she snapped, "Yes, I got it."

There was no way she could *not* get it when he'd spoken so matter-of-factly. She'd never liked being bossed around and he knew that, which was why he'd never done it before. They had understood each other so well. And in the past they'd made decisions together, especially those that defied anyone trying to keep them apart, whether it was her family or his.

But this Bane was difficult to deal with. Didn't he understand it was not in his best interest to go anywhere with her?

Without saying anything else she walked away, leaving him standing in the middle of her living room while she went into the kitchen to check the locks on the back door. She needed time alone. Time away from him. His unexpected arrival had torpedoed her world.

As soon as she was out of his view, she leaned against the kitchen counter and released a sigh as blood pounded through her body. The man she'd loved was back after five years. One moment she'd been rushing around, trying to disappear, and the next she was opening the door for Bane. They had been separated for so long she'd thought... What?

That he wasn't going to come for her. But if she'd really thought that then why hadn't she gotten on with her life?

There were a lot of other whys she needed answered. Why had he decided to become a SEAL? Placing his life at risk with each mission? Better yet, why had he wanted to be involved in something that would keep him from her longer? And why had he shown up today of all days, when her normal life was turned upside down?

On top of everything else, he wanted to take over, as if he'd been here all the time. As if she didn't know what she was doing. As if she hadn't taken care of her own business for the past five years without him.

"Need help in there?" he called out.

Crystal gritted her teeth. "No, I've got this." She crossed the kitchen floor to check the locks on the back door.

What did he expect of her? Of them?

And of all things, within ten minutes of being inside her house they had kissed. A kiss she'd initiated. He might have made the first move by lowering his head, but she had been the one to make the connection. The memory of their mouths locking and tongues tasting had her feeling all hot inside. It had definitely proved they were still attracted to each other. That kiss had snatched all her senses and made her weak in the knees. She was certain she could still taste him on her lips.

She pushed a strand of hair back from her face and walked out of the kitchen and stopped in the living room. Bane's back was to her as he stood in front of her fireplace, staring at the framed photographs on her mantel. Except for one picture of her parents, all the rest were of him or of her and him. Most had been taken when they'd dated and the others when they'd eloped.

He turned around and their gazes met. She almost forgot to breathe. Was that heat in her stomach? And why was her heart beating a mile a minute? She drew in a deep breath wondering what he was thinking. Had he remembered each and every moment in those pictures? Did he remember how in love they'd been? Did he realize, married or not, they were different people now and needed to get to know each other all over again?

Should they?

Could they?

She broke eye contact to look at where her luggage had been. Then she glanced back at him. "You've taken my bags out already?"

"Yes."

"I didn't hear anything. Not even the door open."

A smile tugged at the corner of his lips. "That's the way a SEAL operates."

Oh, God. That smile was turning her insides to mush.

A part of her wanted to race across the room and throw herself in his arms like she used to do. But she couldn't. As far as she was concerned, too much stood in the way, keeping them apart.

Five

"I was sorry to hear about your dad, Crystal," Bane said, after easing the car onto the interstate. "Although the two of us never got along, he was still your father."

He felt her gaze on him, and he wanted to take his eyes off the road and look at her but decided not to. She was gorgeous and every time he gazed at her he felt desire seep into his bones. He needed to keep his self-control so he could convince her that he was coming with her when she left town.

"Thanks. Sending me away to live with Aunt Rachel widened the chasm between us but we made amends before he died…as best we could, considering everything." She was quiet for a moment before continuing, "He even told me he loved me, Bane. And I told him I loved him, as well. Dad leaving me the ranch was a shocker because he said he would be selling it to make sure I never had a reason to return to Denver. But after he died I found out he had left it to me. I wasn't aware he still owned it and assumed he'd sold it like he said he would do."

Bane had assumed Mr. Newsome had sold it, as well. Whenever he came home, Dillon had mentioned that the Newsome place was still deserted, but Bane had assumed the repairs needed around the place hadn't made it an easy sale. But there was something else he'd wanted to tell her. "It's admirable that you're working on your PhD, Crystal. For someone who claimed they hated school, that's quite an accomplishment."

"No big deal. Since I didn't have a life I decided to go to school full-time. All year-round. Nonstop. And when I took a placement test, there were classes I didn't have to take. My parents were happy that I was focusing on my studies again."

And not on him, he thought, and then asked her the question that had nagged at him since he'd first seen her tonight. "How did you do it?"

"Do what?"

"Keep the guys away. You're a very beautiful woman so I'm sure plenty tried hitting on you."

He glanced over and saw the compliment had made her blush. He meant it. She had the kind of beauty he'd never been able to explain with words.

"The guys stayed away because they thought I was gay."

Bane almost swerved into another lane. Placing a tight grip on the steering wheel, he glanced over at her again. "They thought what?"

"That I was gay. I didn't have a boyfriend so what else were they to think? The rumor started in college when I refused all their advances, even the guys on the football team, who were in such high demand on campus. They figured if I wasn't into them, then I must be into females."

"Why didn't you tell them you were a married woman?"

"What good would that have done with a husband who never came around?"

He could imagine how she'd felt knowing a rumor was circulating about her. One that was false.

"I thought about you every day, Crystal."

"Did you?"

He heard the skepticism in her tone. Did she not believe him? He was about to question her when she said, "This isn't the way to the airport, Bane."

"We aren't going to the airport."

"Not going to the airport? And just when did you decide that?"

"When I noticed we were being followed."

They were being followed?

Crystal glanced over at Bane. "How do you know?"

"Because although the driver is trying to be inconspicuous, that blue car has been tailing us for a while."

"Blue car?"

"Yes."

Her muscles trembled. "The car that followed me earlier was blue. But how would he know to follow you when we're not in my car?"

"Evidently someone saw us getting into mine."

The feel of goose bumps moved up her neck. "If the person saw us leave that means he knows where I live."

"Pretty much. But don't worry about it."

His calm unnerved her. How could he tell her not to worry? It was her home they were talking about. Whoever was after her would probably trash her house looking for something that wasn't there.

As if Bane read her mind, he said, "The reason I told you not to worry is because Flip is watching your place for me."

She stared over at him. "Someone you know is watching my house?"

He exited off the interstate. "Yes. David Holloway is one of my team members, who happens to live here in Dallas. His code name is Flipper because he's the best diver on the team. I contacted him when my plane landed to let him know I was in town. I called him again when I took out your luggage. I noticed a strange car in the driveway across the street."

Crystal was trying hard to keep up. He didn't live in her neighborhood, so how could he tell when some car was out of place? "How did you know it was a strange car?"

"I sat in front of your place for two hours waiting for you to come home and it wasn't parked there then," he said, turning another corner.

She noticed they were driving in an area she wasn't familiar with and wondered where in the heck they were going. "That's it? You figured it was out of place because it hadn't been there earlier?"

"That was enough. I'm trained to take stock of my surroundings."

Evidently, she thought. "And this Flipper guy went to my house after we left?"

"He got there just as we were leaving. Flip and his brothers will be keeping an eye on the place while you're gone."

She arched a brow. "Brothers?"

Bane looked over at her when he brought the car to a stop at a traffic light. "Yes, he has four. All SEALs. Your place is in good hands for now."

She was glad to hear that, but she couldn't help wishing the only hands her house was in were hers. Granted, she leased it rather than owned it, but it was the only house she'd lived in since moving to Dallas. When she noticed him glancing in the rearview mirror and grinning she asked, "What's so funny?"

"Ambush. I deliberately had the driver of the blue car follow us here and Flip's brothers were waiting."

"How did they know?"

"When Flip's brothers noticed I was being followed, they followed the blue car. Then one of Flip's brothers passed the blue car and got in the front of us to lead me off the interstate. The others went ahead and were ready to stop the guy at that intersection back there."

Nervousness danced around in her stomach. "So now we can continue to the airport?"

"No," he said, pulling the car into what appeared to be the parking lot of an abandoned warehouse. After parking the car and turning off the lights, he grabbed the mobile phone he'd placed on the dashboard. He glanced down at it for a minute before looking back at her. "There might be others looking for us there."

"Why would you think that?"

He pushed back in the seat to stretch out his legs. "Remember those two men who approached you about coming to work for Homeland Security?"

"Yes, what about them?"

"It seems *they* are the bad guys."

Bane wished he could kiss the shocked look right off Crystal's face, beginning at her eyes and moving slowly downward to her lips.

"That's not possible," she said. "I saw their credentials."

"Whatever credentials they had were faked. The department they claimed to work for under Homeland Security doesn't even exist."

"Are you sure?"

"Positive. I texted a copy of that business card to a friend at Homeland Security and a few minutes ago he verified what I'd suspected."

He watched her nibble her bottom lip and wished seeing her do so didn't have such an arousing effect on him. He had to stay focused. "The mystery of that note bothers me."

"How so?"

"Did the person who wrote it have your best interest at heart, or did he or she advise you to disappear for a reason, hoping when you did it would make it easier for those guys to find you?"

She lifted a brow. "You think someone at Seton Industries, the person who put that note in my desk, is in cahoots with those two guys?"

"You have to admit that's a strong possibility. You said someone broke into your locker. Who would have access to that area other than another employee?"

Bane didn't like this. He and Crystal should be at her place talking about their future and how they would get beyond the five years they'd spent apart.

He started to say something else when his mobile phone rang with Flipper's ringtone. He grabbed it off his dashboard. "What you got, Flip?"

"A bunch of crazies, man. No sooner than you and the blue car pull off, a black sedan pulled up and two goons got out. It was like watching a scene out of *Men in Black* with both of them dressed in black suits and all. Not sure how they planned to break into your wife's place but there's no doubt in my mind that was their intent. Until…"

Bane lifted a brow. "Until what?"

"Until they noticed the infrared beam Mark had leveled in the center of their chests. I guess knowing we could blow their guts out freaked them, especially since we could see them but they couldn't see us. I've never seen two men run back to their car so fast."

Bane shook his head. "You and your brothers are having fun with this, aren't you?"

"Yes, I guess you can say that."

Flip would. Although Bane hadn't met any of Flipper's brothers, he'd heard about them. They had inherited their thirst for excitement and danger from their father, who'd retired as a SEAL. "What about the driver of the blue car?"

"He got out and hauled ass. Left the car running. You said not to shoot anybody so my brothers let him go. Sure you don't want to involve the cops?"

"Not yet." Bane told Flipper about who he figured the men in black were.

"Impersonating government officials isn't good," Flipper said.

Bane had to agree. He glanced over at Crystal and saw she'd been trying to follow his conversation. "You're right. But at least you put the fear of God in them. However, don't be surprised if they come back."

"We'll be ready. Take care of yourself and your lady."

Bane nodded. "I intend to."

He had barely clicked off the phone when Crystal asked, "They broke into my house?"

Her shoulders sagged and he wished he had told Flipper it was okay for his brothers to shoot the bastards after all. He hated that she was going through this. "No, but that had been their intent. Flipper and his brother ran them off." There was no need telling her the method they'd used to do so. "They'll be back if they believe you have information or data stored somewhere in your house."

"I don't."

"I doubt they know that, and the first place they'll look is your computer."

"So what now? Where do we go?"

He checked his watch. It was late. "Find a hotel."

She narrowed her eyes. "Why?"

Not for the reason I want, he thought, again remembering the last time he'd been in a hotel room with her. The memory of her naked on that bed and all they'd been doing before the sheriff had shown up was what had kept him sane during dangerous missions.

"We're going to a hotel to sleep and put a plan of action in place, Crystal. As much as I want to make love to you, I've got a feeling the want isn't mutual."

Which meant it would be a long night.

Six

Crystal broke eye contact with Bane to look out the car window. Of course going to a hotel made sense, but still...

She'd seen the way he'd looked tonight, and she knew that look. Had even fantasized about it a number of times over the years. The memories of what followed that look always made her hot inside. But she wasn't sure she could trust herself alone with him. Her attraction to him was stronger than ever.

"Or we can stay here. Parked," he said, interrupting her thoughts.

She looked over at him. "All night?"

He gave her a smile that had heat swirling in her stomach. "Won't be anything new for us. In fact, it would be just like old times."

Why did he have to go there? Being in a parked car with him would definitely be like old times, but she was no longer a teenager who thought she could never get enough of Bane Westmoreland. She was a woman on the run with a husband she no longer knew. "We're too old for parked cars, Bane."

"I know. That's why I suggested a hotel."

She turned toward him. It was time to burst his bubble. "If we go to a hotel we get separate rooms."

"Why? We're married."

She tried to ignore the sexiness of his voice. And she definitely didn't need to notice the electricity sizzling in the air between them. Yes, they were married, but hadn't it already been established that things had changed? That *they* had changed? For starters, she was no longer a dreamer but a realist. And he was no longer the guy who claimed she would always be his love for life. Apparently the navy had booted her aside.

"Legally yes, we are married, but that's about all. Five years is a long time. We've already established that we're different people now. You may not like the new me, and for all I know I may not like the new you."

"I don't *like* you, Crystal. Never have. I fell in love with you the first time I saw you."

Now, why would he go and say something like that? If he really felt that way, wouldn't he have come back long before now? And why was she now remembering that day when she had been walking home from school, minding her own business, and he'd passed her on his motorcycle. He'd made a U-turn and the moment he'd stopped his bike, taken off his helmet and turned those hazel eyes on her, she'd been lost. So if he wanted to say that he'd fallen in love with her the moment he'd first seen her, she could certainly make that same claim about him.

But there were still those five years apart between them.

"Will it make you feel better if there were two beds in the room?"

Crystal took a breath. *Not really.* Even after being separated for five years she still found him captivating. Even now, tingles of awareness were invading her entire body. She couldn't look at any part of him without getting naughty thoughts. Being in close quarters with him all night would only be asking for trouble. She shook her head. "Doubt that will work, Bane."

He shrugged broad shoulders. "It will have to work, because I don't plan on letting you out of my sight until we get to the bottom of what's going on."

Her gaze narrowed on him. She was about to tell him that when it came to her he didn't make any decisions, when his cell phone went off again. He quickly reached for it. "Yes?"

Crystal studied his face. Whatever the caller was saying was making him angry. She could tell by the fire she saw forming in the depths of his eyes, the tightening of his jaw and the way his fingers gripped the phone. And she couldn't miss the abrasive tone of his voice.

She was certain the call was about her, which was why his gaze flicked to her time and time again. Gone was that hot and steamy I-can't-wait-to-get-some-of-you look in his eyes. It had been replaced with a look that clearly said that if pushed, Brisbane Westmoreland was liable to hurt somebody.

She pushed her hair back from her face and silently tapped her fingers on the car's console. She couldn't wait for the call to end so she could find out what was going on.

As soon as she heard him click off the phone she turned, ready to inquire, but he held up a finger to silence her. Already he had clicked someone else's number. He then quickly barked the words into his phone. "Code purple. Will enlighten everyone in a few."

As soon as he disconnected the call she asked, "What was that about?"

He didn't say anything for a long moment. He just stared at her as if he was trying to make up his mind about something.

She frowned and said, "And don't you dare think about not telling me what's going on, Bane."

Bane had contemplated doing just what she'd accused him of. But he knew he couldn't. Crystal was too intelligent, too quick to figure out things. Besides, she needed to know what they were up against and the caution they would have to take.

But more than anything, he needed her to trust him and to believe that he would never let anyone touch a single hair on her head.

"Bane?"

He took a deep breath. "First, give me your cell phone."

"My cell phone?"

"Yes."

She stared at him for a second, then went into her purse to retrieve her phone. He took it and then got out of the car. Throwing the phone on the pavement and ignoring her shocked gasp, he used his foot to stomp it into pieces.

"Are you crazy? What do you think you're doing?" she asked in outrage after getting out of the car to save her phone. Of course it was too late.

"I'm destroying your phone."

She placed her hands on her hips and glared up at him. "I see that. What I want to know is why."

"There's a chance a tracking device is on it."

"What are you talking about?"

"Things are more serious than I thought or what you might know, Crystal."

She stiffened her spine. "Well, I've got news for you. I don't know anything other than what I received in that note today and that my locker was tampered with and a blue car has been following me."

He glanced around. "Come on, let's get back inside the car. I'll tell you what I know."

She looked down at her smashed phone in disgust before going around the front of the SUV to get back inside. As soon as they had gotten inside the car, she said, "Tell me."

She touched his arm and a surge of desire rushed through him. Evidently it shone in his eyes because she quickly snatched her hand away. "Sorry."

He grabbed her hand, entwined their fingers and met her gaze. "Don't ever apologize for touching me."

Instead of a response, she nervously swiped her tongue across her bottom lip and his own tongue tingled, dying to mate with hers. Since he figured he couldn't kiss her anytime soon, he would tell her what she wanted to know. What she needed to know.

Ignoring the thud in his chest from holding her hand in his, he said, "My contact at Homeland Security did some more digging, even went so far as to tap into classified information. It seems you've been watched for a while."

She lifted a brow. "By who?"

"Mainly the government. They are aware of the research you're working on."

She shrugged. "I figured they were. Seton sent periodic reports to them as part of national security. Besides, the funding for my research was a grant subsidized by the government."

"Well, it seems the report got into the hands of someone it shouldn't have. To make a long story short, a plan was devised to kidnap you and the two other biochemists working on similar projects. They were to take the three of you to a lab underground somewhere and force you to work together and perfect a formula they'd use to their advantage."

Crystal shook her head. "That plan is preposterous."

Bane wished she wouldn't do that. Shake her head and make her hair fan across her face and place more emphasis on her dark eyes. Momentarily he lost his concentration. He couldn't afford any distractions now. There was too much at stake. "Whoever came up with the idea evidently didn't think so. And now you're the missing link."

She leaned back and frowned. "What do you mean I'm the missing link?"

His hand tightened on hers. "The other two chemists were abducted yesterday. One was leaving his home for work and the other chemist was leaving the gym around noon. The plan was to kidnap the three of you within hours of each other. However, their plan to grab you was foiled. But since they are determined to get their hands on the formula, they won't give up."

The spark in her eyes told him she clearly understood what he was saying. She was vital to these guys' plans and they didn't intend to fail. That spark also told him something else. She would like to see them try to grab her. He still had the ability to read her mind sometimes. She still had the spunk he'd always admired in her.

He swallowed hard when she eased her hand from his and broke eye contact to gaze out of the car's windshield. She was thinking, trying to come up with her own plan. One that didn't include him. More for his safety than anything else, he figured. And while she was spending that time thinking, he was spending his time feeling possessive, protective and proactive. If anyone thought they would grab her from him, then they didn't know Bane Westmoreland.

She looked back at him and because he had a feeling he knew what she was about to say, he cut her off before she could start. "I won't leave you unprotected, so forget it."

When she just continued to look at him, he added, "I need you to trust my ability to keep us safe."

A ripple of awareness floated between them and he tried to ignore it. Knowing he had her trust was more important at the moment.

"It's going to be hard, Bane," she said softly. "I've been on my own for a long time."

Five years. And not for the first time he wondered if he'd done the right thing in staying away. She had been his wife, yet he'd left her believing that living apart was the best thing for both of them. That they'd both needed to grow up and mature. Especially him. And he had. But what if he hadn't shown up today? What if she'd gotten kidnapped like those other two chemists? What if—

"I will trust you in this, Bane."

Her words intruded into his thoughts. He nodded. He was more than ready to be the husband she deserved, but he had to show her that she could trust him. Not just to keep her safe, but to build a life with her.

"So…" she said with a heavy sigh. "What now?"

A smile touched his lips. "Now we show them that together we're a force to reckon with."

A force to reckon with.

Crystal couldn't help but smile. That was how Sheriff Harper used to describe them. Nothing, not even the threat of jail time, could keep Bane from her or her from him. They'd been that fixated on each other.

Bane's cell phone signaled a text massage had come through and he grabbed the phone off the dashboard. Out the car window she saw they were parked in an unlit area. The only illumination was from the stars and moon overhead. Bane read the text with his full attention while her full attention was on him. She couldn't help but admire the way his wide shoulders fit his leather jacket and the casual way he sat in his seat. He had pushed the seat back to accommodate his long legs. And speaking of those long legs...

She loved how they looked bare, whenever he went swimming, and when they were covered in jeans, like they were now. Or when he rode his motorcycle or one of the horses from his family ranch. She'd known how to ride when she met him, but with his help, she had perfected the skill. He'd also taught her how to ride a motorcycle, shoot a gun and climb mountains. She had shared his love for the outdoors and they would spend time together outside whenever they could.

She swept her gaze over him from head to toe, thinking he was definitely sheer male perfection, the epitome of every woman's fantasy. It was only when he'd cleared his throat that she realized he had finished reading the text and had caught her ogling him.

"Yes? Did you say something?"

He chuckled. "No. Just wanted you to know that our ride will be here in a few minutes."

She lifted a brow. "Our ride?"

"Yes. We're changing vehicles. Chances are the people looking for you have already ID'd this one, so we need to swap it out."

"So who's bringing us another vehicle?" she asked,

glancing out the window. Other than a huge vacant building, the parking lot was empty.

"Flip's dad."

She frowned. "His dad?"

"Yes. He's an ex-SEAL."

Moments later Crystal heard the sound of another vehicle pull up and noted the driver had turned out the headlights. Bane looked over at her.

"That's our ride."

Seven

Bane gathered their belongings out of the SUV so they could place them in the trunk of the car Mr. Holloway had delivered.

Flip favored his father. Same shade of blue eyes and blond hair, although the older man had streaks of gray. It was easy to tell the man had been a SEAL. A commanding officer. He was still alert and wore an intense look on his face. And it was quite obvious that even at the age of sixty-five, he was in great shape physically. He was ready for anything and could probably still hold his own.

"Don't need to know where you're headed. The less people who know the better. Just be safe," the older man said, handing Bane the keys.

"I will, and thanks for everything, Mr. Holloway. I owe you and your family."

Mr. Holloway waved off his words. "No, you don't.

David told me and his brothers what happened during your last mission when you saved his life. Besides, any friend of my boys is a friend of mine. If you get in a pinch, just give us a call."

Bane didn't plan on getting in a pinch, but figured it was best to accept the offer just the same. "I will, and thanks."

Crystal was already seated inside the new car with her seat belt snapped in place. The older man followed Bane's gaze. "I understand that's your wife who you haven't seen in a while."

Bane nodded as he looked back at the man. "Yes, that's right."

"And she waited for you to come back for all that time?"

Bane nodded, remembering what Crystal had told him. She had kept her promise like he'd kept his. "Yes, she waited."

The older man smiled. "Then, you're a very lucky man. Take care of yourself and your wife."

His wife. He liked the sound of that. He was ready to finally claim her as his wife—but he had to keep her safe first. "I will. Again, thanks for all you and your sons have done. Are still doing." He knew Flip and his brothers would be keeping an eye on Crystal's place for a while.

"Don't mention it." Mr. Holloway gave him a supportive pat on the shoulder before getting into the SUV to drive off.

Bane quickly walked to the car, got inside, closed the door and locked it.

Crystal glanced over at him. "Where to now?"

He could hear the exhaustion in her voice. It was close to eleven. Probably past her bedtime. "A hotel, but not here in Dallas. Get some sleep. We'll be riding for a while."

"Okay."

She didn't ask where they were headed and as he started the ignition, he watched her lower her seat into a reclining position. He couldn't stop his appreciative gaze from sweeping over her, taking in how the denim molded to her hips and thighs. At eighteen she'd had a slender figure. Now she was amazingly curvy with a small waist. Forcing his eyes off her, he adjusted the car's temperature to a comfortable setting. It had gotten pretty cold outside.

As he pulled out of the parking lot he saw her starting to doze off. She looked just as beautiful with her eyes closed as she did when they were open. This was what he had dreamed about, what he had craved. The two of them together again.

Bane had driven a few miles and had made it to their first traffic light when he heard the sound of her chuckle. He glanced over at her and saw that her eyes were closed, yet a smile had formed on her lips. Was she having a dream or something? No sooner had that thought entered his mind than she opened her eyes, saw him looking at her and shifted upright in her seat. "What's wrong?" she asked.

"Nothing is wrong with me. You chuckled in your sleep just now."

A smile touched her lips. "I wasn't asleep. Just resting my eyes. And I got to thinking that this is getting to be the norm for us."

"What?"

"Being on the run. The last time we were together we eloped and were running from Sheriff Harper. Remember?"

"Yes, I remember." How could he forget? They had intentionally led everyone on a wild-goose chase thinking they were headed to Vegas when they'd married in Utah.

"Now we're on the run from heaven knows who."

"Doesn't matter. We're together again," he said.

She didn't say anything, and when the traffic light changed, he moved forward. After a while he figured she'd dozed off…or as she put it, had gone back to resting her eyes, when she asked, "For how long, Bane?"

Grateful for another traffic light, he brought the car to a stop and glanced over at her. "How long?"

"Yes, how long will we be together before you leave? Before I'm all alone again? You're a SEAL. That means you'll be gone a lot, right?"

He hesitated for a moment, giving thought to how he would respond. If she thought he would allow her to use his being a SEAL against him, against them, then she was definitely wrong. "Yes, I might be gone on missions whenever my CO calls."

"Your CO?"

"Commanding officer."

"And what if he calls now? You'll have to go, won't you?"

He tightened his grip on the steering wheel. Was she trying to insinuate that when it came to her he wasn't dependable? "Unless there's a national threat of some kind, it won't happen. I'm on military leave. My entire team is."

"Why?"

Now, this was where things got kind of sticky. He had to let her know that parts of his job weren't up for discussion, but he'd save that heart-to-heart conversation for later. Right now he merely said, "We were due one." That was the truth, although he wasn't telling her everything.

"You take risks. Put your life in danger."

Now it was his turn to chuckle.

"What's so funny?" she asked.

"I was just thinking that right now it's not my life that's in danger. I'd say we both have unusual occupations."

"There's nothing unusual about mine. I just happen to be working on research that's pretty sensitive."

He smiled, figuring that was one way of looking at it. "I guess you can say I work on things that are pretty sensitive, as well."

"There's no comparing what we do so don't even try, Bane."

Okay, so she had a point. But still, like he'd told her, he wasn't the one in danger now. "I'm well trained in what I do. Six months ago I made master sniper." That had been a major accomplishment for someone who was new on the team. But Bane's skills as a sharpshooter were what had caught the eye of his chief in boot camp. When he discovered Bane could hit a bull's-eye target with one eye closed, the man had put the thought of becoming a SEAL in Bane's head. The chief had made the captain aware of Bane's skill and the captain had pulled a lot of strings to get him into the naval academy.

"Master sniper? That doesn't surprise me. You were the one who taught me and Bailey how to shoot. And you always held your own against JoJo."

Yes, he had, he remembered proudly. And the Westmorelands sure knew how to shoot. He hadn't been surprised when he'd gotten home and everyone had told him about that grizzly bear Bailey had taken down in Alaska last month. And Crystal had been just as good a shot as Bailey. Only person better than those two was JoJo, who was now married to his brother Stern.

"And you want me to think your job isn't dangerous, Bane?"

"I admit it's dangerous, but it's also rewarding."

He heard her snort before she said, "I can see you think it's rewarding because it gives you an excuse to kick ass in the name of your country."

He laughed, and considering everything, it felt good to laugh. Especially with her. She always had a knack for bringing humor to any situation, although he was convinced what she'd just said hadn't been meant to be funny.

"You're making a career out of it, though, aren't you?"

Was she seriously asking or did she think she had everything figured out already? "Not sure. It's a decision we will have to make together."

"Oh, no, don't pull me into this, Bane. I won't let you blame me for making your life miserable."

Making his life miserable? What was she talking about? "Define what you mean."

"Gladly. I can see you as a SEAL, and a darn good one. What I don't see is you going into the office at Blue Ridge Management every day. You'd go stark crazy sitting behind a desk. And you'd never forgive me if you saw me as the reason you had to go work there."

She knew him well and was right about his not wanting to work at his family's company. Although his brothers—Dillon, Riley, Canyon and Stern—as well as his cousin Aidan were a perfect fit for Blue Ridge Land Management, he wasn't.

"I could join Jason, Derringer and Zane in their horse-training business," he said. Honestly, he couldn't imagine doing that, either. He didn't have the same love of horses that his brother and two cousins had.

"Bailey told me about their company the last time we talked."

"But she wouldn't tell you anything about me," he said in a gruff tone.

Crystal frowned at him. "That was the rule, Bane, and need I remind you that it was your idea." She broke eye contact with him to glance out the side window.

Yes, it had been. And it was time they talked about it. He suddenly felt the tension flowing in the car between them and didn't like it. "You know why I made my decision, Crystal."

"The decision to desert me?"

He quickly swerved off the road and whipped into the parking lot of what looked like an all-night truck stop. He pulled in between two tractor trailers, which concealed them from the view of anyone driving by. He brought the car to a stop and turned off the ignition.

"Are you trying to kill us, Bane?" she asked, trying to catch her breath.

Instead of answering, he unsnapped his seat belt and turned toward her. "I know you didn't just say that I deserted you."

Crystal could tell Bane was furious. She'd seen him angry before, but his anger had never been directed at her. Now it was. He was glaring at her to the point where the color of his eyes seemed to take on a Saint Patrick's Day green. But she had a feeling it was not her lucky day. Not backing down, she lifted her chin. "And what if I did?"

"Then, we need to talk."

"Too late for that. Nothing you say will make me change the way I feel."

"Then, you need to tell me why you feel that way."

He really didn't know? She would find the whole thing amusing but instead she wanted to cry. She had loved him so much. He had been her world. The yang to her yin. The one person she'd thought would never hurt her or let her down. But he had.

"Crystal?"

Fine, if he wanted to pretend he didn't know why she felt the way she did then she'd tell him. "I understand why you let my father send me away after we eloped but—"

"It was for the best. You were going to drop out of school, Crystal. I couldn't let you do that. I couldn't interfere with your education. It was November. All you had to do was make it to June to graduate."

"I know all that," she snapped. "So I let my father think he was calling the shots when he sent me to live with Aunt Rachel." The memory of that day still scorched her brain whenever she thought about it. "I figured I could put up with it because you would come and get me in June after I finished high school."

She saw the look in his eyes, knew the exact moment he figured out where she was going with this. She took a deep breath and plunged forward. "When you finally called me in January, I thought it was to tell me you couldn't live without me and had decided to come for me early. And that I could finish school back in Denver while we lived together in the cabin you had built for me. As man and wife."

"Dammit, Crystal, I know you. If I had come for you early, you would have come up with all kinds of excuses not to go back to school. Plus, I wouldn't have been able to support you. I wasn't old enough to claim my land or my trust fund. When I finished high school, my income came from working odd jobs. I walked off the job Dillon gave me at Blue Ridge at the end of the first week. I didn't like my supervisor telling me what to do. I was a Westmoreland. My family owned the damn company and I figured that gave me the right to do whatever the hell I wanted."

"I would have gone back to school, Bane. I promised you that I would. And as far as you not having a stable income, we would have made it work."

"You deserved more."

"I thought I deserved you. I was your wife."

"Why can't you understand that I needed to make something of myself?" he asked in an agitated tone. "As your husband, I owed that to you. Why can't you see that you deserved better than what I was at the time? I was an undisciplined man without any goals in life. I enjoyed defying authority."

"Those things didn't matter to me, Bane."

"They should have."

She narrowed her gaze at him. "Your family got to you, didn't they? Convinced you we didn't belong together. So you told no one we were married. No one but Bailey."

She watched him rub his hands down his face in frustration. As far as she was concerned, he had no right to be frustrated. She was the one he'd forgotten about when he'd chosen a career as a SEAL over her.

"You're wrong about my family, Crystal. They knew how much I loved you, but they saw what we refused to see. They knew we couldn't keep going the way we were headed. So I made a decision that I felt was best for us. And I want to believe that it was. Look at you now.

You not only finished high school, but you went on to college and got your master's degree and are working on your PhD. You were always smart and I was holding you back. Had I been selfish enough to claim you as my wife, I would have taken you to that cabin and made a pitiful life for you there. And it would have been just our luck if you'd gotten pregnant. What sort of future would our kid have had?"

She quickly turned her face away so he wouldn't see the tears in her eyes, but she hadn't been quick enough. Bane knew her. He could read her when she didn't want to be read. And she knew he was doing it now when he reached out, used his finger to turn her face back toward him. He studied her features intently.

Moments later he narrowed his gaze. "What's wrong? What aren't you telling me, Crystal?"

She knew she had to tell him. There was no reason to keep her secret any longer. "That day when you called and told me you had decided to go into the navy, you asked me if I was pregnant and I told you no."

He didn't say anything for a minute and a part of her knew he'd already guessed what she was about to say. "But you lied, didn't you? You *were* pregnant, weren't you?" he said in an accusing tone.

She didn't say anything for a long moment and then answered, "I didn't lie. When you asked, I wasn't pregnant…any longer. I had miscarried our baby, Bane. A few days before. The day you called was the day Aunt Rachel brought me home from the hospital."

Eight

Bane literally buckled over as if he'd been kicked in the gut. In a way he had. He drew in a deep breath as if doing so would ease the pain. It took a few moments for him to get himself together, and when he looked over at Crystal, she was sitting up straight in her car seat and the first thing he noticed were the tears streaming down her face.

His breath caught. He'd always been a sucker for tears…especially hers. But a part of him couldn't ignore that she'd been pregnant with their child and hadn't told him. Although he hadn't known where her parents had sent her, other than to live with some aunt, she had known how to reach him. And she hadn't even tried.

He recalled the days he had waited by the phone, figuring she would get around to contacting him somehow to let him know where she was. And when she hadn't, he'd figured her parents had probably talked the same sense into her that Dillon had talked into him. It was then and only then, that he had made the decision to follow Dillon's advice and make something of himself before going to claim her.

Trying to pull himself together and keep the anger out of his voice, he asked, "How could you not tell me?"

She looked over at him. "I didn't tell you because you'd already made up your mind about what you wanted to do."

"Dammit, Crystal, I only went into the navy because—"

"You thought I deserved more. You've said that."

A muscle in his jaw ticked. When had she developed such a damn attitude? He felt anger beginning to roll around in his stomach and he worked hard to control it because he'd never lost his temper with her. "Yes, I said it and I will keep on saying it."

Neither of them spoke for a while and the silence between them was thick, full of the tension he knew they both felt. "When did you know you were pregnant?" he finally asked her.

Tears reappeared in her eyes and she swiped them away. "That's the thing, Bane. I didn't know. I was late but I'd been late before, you know that. So I really didn't think anything about it. I was trying to fit into a new school and was focusing on my studies. It was nearing the end of January and I was looking forward to you coming to get me by June. Silly me, I figured even if you didn't know where I was that you would look for me until you found me.

"Anyway, I got really bad stomach pains one night. When I went to the bathroom I noticed I was bleeding profusely and woke up my aunt. She took me to the emergency room and after checking me over, the doctor told me I'd been pregnant and had lost the baby.

They kept me in the hospital overnight because I'd lost a lot of blood."

She swiped at her eyes again. "How can a woman be pregnant and not know it? How could I have carried your baby—our baby—in my body and not know it? That seemed so unfair, Bane. So unfair. The doctor was a nice woman. She said miscarriages weren't uncommon and usually happen within the early weeks of pregnancy. I figured I'd gotten pregnant on our wedding night so I was less than eight weeks along. She assured me it wasn't because of anything I did, and that my next pregnancy should go smoothly."

A deep pain sliced through Bane. It had been his baby as well, and at that moment he mourned for the loss of a life that would never be. A baby that had been a part of him and a part of her. He wanted to reach out and pull Crystal into his arms. Hold her. Share the pain. He felt he had every right to do that. But then he also felt she'd put an invisible wall between them and he would need to tear it down, piece by piece.

"I'm sorry about our baby," he said, meaning every word. It was true he'd gotten careless on their wedding night. It had been the first time they'd ever spent the entire night together, wrapped in each other's arms, and he had been so overjoyed he'd gotten carried away and hadn't used a condom. "I never deserted you, Crystal. I could no more do that than cut off my arm. Do you have any idea what I went through when we were apart?" he asked softly. "How much I suffered each day not knowing where you were?"

"I called you."

"When?"

"As soon as I could get away from my parents. They kept an eye on me during the entire plane trip to South

Carolina, but when the plane landed I went into the ladies' room and asked some woman to use her cell phone. It was around five hours after we parted."

Bane frowned. He hadn't gotten her call. But then he figured it out. "I know the reason why you couldn't reach me," he said, remembering that day. "I was at the cabin, and there's no phone reception out there."

He paused and then added, "After Sheriff Harper told me you'd left Denver, I stormed out of the police station and got into my truck and went to your parents' place and found it deserted. I drove around awhile, getting angrier by the minute. Somehow I ended up at the cabin and I stayed there for two whole days. On the third day Riley came and convinced me to go home with him."

She nodded. "That's probably why I still couldn't reach you the next night, either. I waited until everyone had gone to bed and sneaked downstairs and used my aunt's phone. I couldn't get you, which was just as well because Dad caught me trying. He got upset all over again, and said he knew I would try calling you and figured it was time for me to know the truth."

Bane frowned. "What truth?"

"That he and your brother Dillon had met when we first went missing and made a deal."

"What kind of a deal?"

"The two of them agreed that when we were found, Dillon would keep you away from me and Dad was to keep me away from you."

"That's a damn lie!" Bane said bluntly, feeling red-hot anger flow through him.

"How can you be so sure?"

Her question only infuriated him more. "First of all, Dil doesn't operate that way. Second, Dillon wasn't even in Denver when we eloped. He was somewhere in Wyoming following up on leads to learn more about my great-grandfather Raphel. Ramsey called Dil but he didn't get home until after we were found."

Bane angrily rubbed his hand over his head. "I can't believe you fell for what your dad said. You knew how much he despised the Westmorelands. Did you honestly think he and Dillon sat down and talked about anything?"

She lifted her chin. "I didn't want to believe it but…"

"But what?"

"I called you twice and you didn't take my calls."

"I didn't take them because I didn't get them," he said.

"Well, I didn't know that."

"You should have."

"Well, I didn't. And when you finally called me… two months later…it was to tell me you were going into the navy and it would be best for us to go our separate ways."

His frown deepened. "The reason it was two months later was because it took me that long to find out where you'd gone. And Bailey had to pickpocket your dad's phone to find out then. And as far as saying it was best for us to go our separate ways, that's *not* what I said."

"Pretty much sounded like it to me."

Had it? Frustrated, he leaned back in his seat, trying to recall what he'd said. Joining the navy had been a hard decision, but he'd made it after talking to his cousin Dare, who'd been in the marines. He'd also talked to Riley's best friend Pete. Pete's brother, Matthew, had joined the navy a few years before, and Pete had told Bane how much money Matthew had saved and how the military had trained him to work on aircrafts. Bane had figured going into the navy would not only teach him a skill but also get him out of Denver for a while. Being there without Crystal had made him miserable.

As he recalled all he'd said to her that day, he could see why she'd assumed it was a break-up call, considering the lie her father had told her. His only saving grace had been the promises he'd made to her that he would keep his wedding vows and would come back for her. That made him wonder...

"You think I deserted you. Did you not believe me when I told you that I would come for you once I made something of myself? And that I would keep my wedding vows?" he asked.

She glanced out the window before looking over at him. "Yes, at the time I believed you, although I sort of resented you for putting me out of your life even for a little while, for whatever the reason."

Her words took him by surprise. How could she think he would do such a thing? And she had said, "at the time I believed you." Did that mean at some point in time she had stopped believing? Now he wondered if he'd made a grave mistake not keeping the lines of communication open between them.

"I never put you out of my life and I had every intention of coming back for you. That never changed, Crystal. I thought about you every day. Sometimes every hour, minute and second. I longed for you. I went to bed every night needing you. There were days when I wasn't sure I could go on without you and wanted to give up. That's why I made sure Bailey didn't tell me where you were. Had I known, I would have given up for sure and come after you. And had you told me about your miscarriage, nothing would have stopped me from coming for you. Navy or no navy."

Unable to stop himself, he released his seat belt and reached out and unfastened hers before pulling her across the console to hold her in his arms.

Crystal buried her face in Bane's chest. She couldn't stop her tears from flowing and was surprised she had any tears left to shed. She'd figured she had gone through all of them when the doctor had broken the news to her that day that she had lost her baby. And then getting Bane's call, the same day she'd come home from the hospital, had been too much.

Her aunt Rachel had been wonderful and understanding, the one to hold Crystal each time she wept. And when she'd begged her aunt not to tell her parents about the baby, her aunt had given Crystal her word that she wouldn't. Whether it had been his intention or not, his phone call that day had made her feel as if he was turning his back on them and their love. Deserting her. It had been her aunt who had persuaded her to pull herself together and make decisions about her life...with or without Bane. So she had made them without him. But each time Bailey had called after that, a part of her had hoped it was Bane instead of his cousin. Then, when it had gotten too much for her to deal with, she'd had her number changed.

After listening to Bane's words just now, she remembered all too well how she had thought about him every day, sometimes every hour, minute and second, as well. He had longed for her, gone to bed needing her, and she had done the same for him. At one point she had been tempted to go to Denver to find him. But then she'd known he wouldn't be there and hadn't a clue where he would be. And at some point, how had he expected her not to doubt he still cared when he hadn't contacted her in five years?

"I'm fine now, Bane," she said, pushing back from him and wiping away her tears.

He looked down at her with an intense scrutiny that sent shivers through her body. "Are you, Crystal? Are you fine? Or will you hold it against me for wanting to give you the best of me?"

"I thought I already had the best of you, Bane. You didn't hear me complaining, did you?"

He didn't say anything and she used that time to scramble out of his lap and back into her seat. She stared out the window and could see from the reflection in the glass that he was staring at her.

Without turning back around to him, she asked, "Have you decided where we're going?"

He started the ignition. "Yes, I know where we're going."

Instead of telling her where, he pulled the car out of the parking spot and headed back to the main road.

Nine

"I'll take the bed closer to the door, Crystal," Bane said, dropping his luggage on the floor by the bed.

Instead of answering him, she merely nodded and rolled her luggage over to the other bed. Figuring that she had missed dinner, he'd stopped at an all-night diner to grab orders of chicken and waffles. Then he had driven four hours before finally settling at this hotel for the night. During that time she hadn't said one word to him, not a one. And her silence bothered the hell out of him. How could she be upset with him for wanting to give her a better life? How could she think he'd deserted her? It now seemed that not keeping in contact with her had been a mistake, but what she failed to understand was that she was his weakness.

She said she would have been satisfied with him just the way he was. Flaws and all. But she deserved more. Deserved better. No matter what she thought, he would always believe that. He would admit he had been separated from her longer than he'd planned, and for that he would take the blame. Five years was a long time to expect her to put her life on hold. But that was just it. He hadn't expected her to put her life on hold. He had expected her to make something worthwhile out of it, like he had been doing with his. And she had. She had finished high school, earned both bachelor and master's degrees and was now working on her PhD. All during the five years he'd been gone. Why couldn't she understand that when he'd decided to go into the navy, he'd believed that he was giving them both the chance to be all that they could be, while knowing in the end they would be together? They would always be together. Although he'd loved her more than life, he had been willing to make the sacrifice. Why hadn't she? Had he been wrong to assume that no matter what, their love would be strong enough to survive anything? Even a long separation?

"I need to take a shower."

His heart nearly missed a beat upon hearing the sound of her voice again. At least she was back to talking to him. "All right. I figure we'll check out after breakfast and head south."

"South?"

"Yes, but that might change depending on any reports I get from people I have checking on a few things."

"Is that what that Code Purple was all about?"

So she had been listening. "Yes. That's a code for my team. It means one of us is in trouble and all hands on deck."

"Oh, I see."

She then opened her luggage and dismissed him again. He placed his own travel bag on the bed and opened it. The first thing he came to was the satchel containing all the cards and letters he'd saved for her over the years. He had looked forward to finally giving them to her. But now...

"You haven't heard anything else about my home, have you?"

He looked over at her. Although she'd taken several naps while he'd been driving, she still looked tired and exhausted. However, fatigued or not, to him she looked beautiful. "No. Flip has everything under control."

She nodded before gathering a few pieces of clothing under her arms and heading for the bathroom, closing the door behind her. Deciding he would really try hard to not let her attitude affect his, he took the satchel and walked over to place it on her bed. It was hers. He had kept it for her and had lived for years just waiting for the day when he could give it to her. He wouldn't let the bitterness she felt keep him from giving it to her.

His phone beeped, letting him know he'd received a text message. He glanced at his watch. It was two in the morning. He pulled his phone from his jacket and read Flip's message. All quiet here.

He texted back. Let's hope things stay that way.

He tried to ignore the sound of running water. He could just imagine Crystal stripping off her clothes for her shower. He would love being in there with her, taking pleasure in stepping beneath the spray of water with her, lathering her body and then making love to her. He would press her against the wall, lift her up so her legs encircled his waist and then he would ease inside her. How many nights had he lain in bed and fantasized of doing that very thing?

To take his mind off his need to make love to his wife, he glanced around the hotel room, checking things out in case they needed to make a quick get-away. This room was definitely a step up from the one they'd shared on their wedding night. He'd taken her to a nice enough hotel in Utah, but tonight's room was more spacious. The beds looked warm and inviting and the decor eye-catching.

Crystal had accompanied him inside when he'd booked the room. He could feel her body tense up be-side him when he'd told the hotel clerk he wanted one room. He'd then heard her sigh of relief when he'd added that he wanted a room with two beds.

He lifted a brow when his cell phone went off and he recognized the ringtone. It was a call from home. Dil-lon. He pulled his phone out of his back pocket again. "Yes, Dil?"

"You didn't call to let us know you'd made it to Dal-las. Is everything okay?"

How could he tell his brother that no, everything wasn't okay? "Yes, I made it to Dallas. Sorry, I didn't call but things got kind of crazy."

"Crazy? Were you able to find Crystal?"

"Yes, went straight to her place but…"

"But the warm, cozy, loving reception that you had expected isn't what you got."

He shook his head. His brother could say that again. "I figured we would have to work through some issues, but I didn't expect her to open the door with a loaded gun in her hand, her luggage packed and a bunch of bad guys trying to kidnap her."

There was a pause and then Dillon said, "I think you need to start from the beginning, Bane."

Crystal toweled herself off and tried not to think of the man on the other side of the door. The man she had shared her first kiss with. Her body. The man who had been her best friend. The one who'd defied her father's threat of jail time just to be with her. And the man who was her husband.

She glanced at herself in the mirror. Did Bane see the changes? Did he like what he saw? She couldn't attribute her figure to spending time in the gym or anything. The changes had just happened. One day she was thin and then the next, right after she'd turned twenty, the curves had come. The guys at college had noticed it, too, and tried causing problems. That was when she wished she'd had a wedding ring on her finger that would have deterred their interest. Instead, she had this, she thought, glancing at her locket.

She brought it to her lips and kissed it. It had been what had kept her sane over the past five years. She would look at it and think of Bane and remember the promise. Even on those days she hadn't wanted to remember or thought he'd possibly forgotten.

Her heart began thumping in her chest when she recalled how he had looked at her a few times tonight. The last had been when she'd told him she was going to take a shower. Nobody could turn her on quicker with a mere look than Brisbane Westmoreland. When he had leveled those hazel eyes on her, she could feel her skin get flushed. He was the only one in his family with that eye color, which he'd inherited from his great-grandmother.

She slid into a pair of sweats and then pulled on an oversize T-shirt. Looking into the mirror again, she nervously licked her lips as she thought of Bane. *What a man. What a man*. She even used her hands to fan herself. A number of times on the ride tonight she had pretended to be asleep just so she could study him without him knowing she was doing so. If his eyes weren't bad enough, he had an adorable set of lashes. Almost too long to be a man's. He had taken off his jacket and she couldn't help but appreciate the breadth of his shoulders. Bane was so well toned that it was obvious he lifted weights or something. SEALs were known to stay in shape. If it was required of them, then he was passing that test with flying colors.

Knowing she had spent more time than she needed in the bathroom, she gathered up her clothes in her arms and slowly opened the door. She saw Bane sitting at the desk staring at a laptop.

A laptop? How many times in the past when she'd tried showing him how to surf the net had he claimed he was technology challenged and just couldn't get the hang of using a computer? She sniffed the air and picked up the smell of coffee. Evidently he'd made a pot while she was taking a shower. Coffee was something she'd never acquired the taste for. She preferred hot chocolate or herbal tea.

Crystal cleared her throat. "I'm finished."

"Okay."

He didn't even turn around, but kept his back to her as he stared at the computer screen. Shoving the clothes she'd taken off earlier into the small travel laundry bag, she turned to put it into her luggage and saw the satchel on the bed. She picked it up. "You left something on my bed."

It was then that he looked over his shoulder at her and at that moment she wished he hadn't. Having those hazel eyes trained on her was sending spikes of desire up her spine. "I put it there. It's yours."

She lifted a brow. "Mine?"

"Yes." He turned back to his computer.

She glanced down at the satchel. "What's in it?"

Without turning back around to her he said, "Why don't you look inside and see?"

Bane returned his attention to the computer screen, or at least he pretended to. He'd known the moment Crystal had walked out of the bathroom. Hearing the door open had sent all kinds of arousing sensations through him. The last thing he needed was to glance over at her. His control wasn't all that great. Going without her for five years was playing havoc on his brain cells. Although he kept his eyes glued to the computer, he could hear her ease the leather strap of his satchel open. His wife never could resist her curiosity, and he'd known it.

"There are cards in here. A lot of cards and envelopes," he heard her say. Yet he still refused to turn around.

"Yes. I remembered your birthday, our wedding anniversary, Valentine's Day and Christmas every year. Although I couldn't mail them to you, I bought them anyway and tucked them inside my satchel. I knew one day, when we got back together again, I'd have them for you."

He could hear her shuffling through all those sealed envelopes. "There are letters in here, as well," she said.

"Yes. Most of the other guys had wives or significant others to write home to, but again, I couldn't do the same for you. So I got in the habit of writing you a letter whenever you weighed heavily on my mind." He hoped she could tell from the number of letters he'd written that she'd consumed his mind a lot of the time.

"Thanks, Bane. This is a surprise. I hadn't expected you to do this...for me."

This time he couldn't help but turn around when he said, "I would do just about anything for you, Crystal."

It never ceased to amaze him how easily he could make her blush. At least that hadn't changed. He could actually feel her gaze moving across his face as she held his stare and he wondered if she could feel him doing the same thing. Suddenly, she broke eye contact with him while drawing in a deep breath. He could see the nipples of her breasts pressing against the T-shirt she had on. It was supposed to fit large on her, but she still looked sexy as hell wearing it.

She glanced back down at the satchel. "I can't wait to read the cards and letters."

He nodded and then turned his attention back to his laptop just when the shrill ring of his mobile phone got his attention. He grabbed it off the desk. "This is Bane."

He nodded and his jaw tightened as he listened to what his friend was telling him. Nick Stover, who used to be a member of his SEAL team, had decided to leave the field and go work for Homeland Security when his wife gave birth to triplets. Bane appreciated his friend's inside scoop. But what he was telling him now had his temper rising.

When Nick was done, Bane said, "Okay. Thanks for letting me know so I can get in touch with Flip."

He clicked off the phone and immediately called Flipper. There was no doubt Crystal had stopped whatever she was doing to listen to his conversation. He would have to tell her what was going on. But first, he had a question for her. He turned around and saw her staring at him.

"Is there anything in your home you want saved?"

She frowned. "What?"

"I asked if there's anything in your house that you want to save."

He could tell by the look on Crystal's face that she was trying to figure out why he would ask her such a thing. Before he could explain himself further, he heard Flip pick up the phone. "This is Bane." He knew Nick had already relayed the same information to Flip that he'd just told him.

"Yes, there are some things she wants to save." Since Crystal hadn't answered his question, just continued to look at him like he'd grown a set of horns or something, he said to Flip, "I know for certain she'll want to save all the photographs on her fireplace mantel."

Crystal crossed the room to stand next to him. "Hold it! Why are you telling him that, Bane? What's happening to my house?"

Bane spoke into the phone. "I'll call you back in a sec, Flip." He then clicked off the phone and placed it back on the desk.

He regretted having to answer her question, but knew he had to. "In a couple of hours or so, your house will get burned down to the ground."

Ten

Crystal felt the room spinning and wondered if she was about to fall flat on her face. Bane was obviously wondering the same thing because he was out of his chair in a flash and had grabbed hold of her arm to steady her.

"I think you need to sit down, Crystal," he said, trying to ease her down into the chair he'd just vacated.

"No. I won't sit down," she said, telling herself she'd just imagined what he'd said about her house burning down. There was no way he could have said that. But all it took was to see the concerned look on his face to know she hadn't imagined anything at all.

"Why would anyone want to burn my house down?" She just couldn't fathom such a thing.

"Actually, it's not just anyone. The order came from Homeland Security."

Shock took over her features. "Homeland Security? Why would the government do something like that?"

"I told you about those other two chemists who were kidnapped. And now the kidnappers are trying to get their hands on you. It's a serious situation, Crystal, and you're talking about national security. As long as there's a possibility something is in your house connected to the project you're working on, then—"

"But I told you there wasn't. I never bring work home."

"The Department of Homeland Security can't take any chances. Without you the bad guys will try to piece together what they need, and DHS can't let them do that."

"Fine. Get them on the phone."

"Get who on the phone?"

"Someone at Homeland Security. Evidently you have their number. If they don't believe you, then maybe they will believe me."

"I can't do that."

"Why not?"

There was a moment of silence before he said, "Because right now we can't trust anyone. Not even Homeland Security. At least until they find out what's going on. Evidently, there's a mole within the organization. Otherwise, how else would your project come under such close scrutiny?"

He moved around her to the cabinet that held the coffeepot, poured a cup and took a sip. He leaned back against the cabinet and added, "Homeland Security has no idea where you are. All they know is the bad guys haven't nabbed you yet because they're still trying to find you. Obviously, the person who sent you that note is one of the good guys and figured out what was about to go down, which is why he or she told you to disappear. For all they know, that's what you did."

He took another sip of his coffee. "So beside those framed photographs over your fireplace, is there anything else in your house you want to save?"

Crystal drew in a deep breath. Technically, it wasn't her house since she was leasing it. But it was where she'd made a home for the past year, putting her own signature on it with the decorating she'd done. What she'd liked most about her home was the screened-in patio. She could sit out there for hours and read. That made her realize that all the furniture she did own would probably be destroyed because it was too big to move out without attracting attention. The impact of that made her slide down in the chair. It was still warm from when Bane had sat in it.

"We don't have much time, Crystal."

She sat upright, glad she'd already packed her marriage license and placed it inside the photo album she'd kept for Bane. "My family Bible," she said with resolve. "It's in the nightstand drawer. And there are more pictures in a small trunk under my bed."

"Okay."

He returned to the desk and when he reached for his phone, his arm brushed against hers. The feel of their skin coming into contact made her draw in a sharp breath. He looked at her, holding her gaze for a minute, and she knew he'd felt the sizzle, as well. He continued to hold her gaze, letting her know she had his full attention while he talked on the phone. "Flip, check the nightstand drawer next to her bed and grab her family Bible. And there's a small trunk under her bed."

Moments later he clicked off the phone. "I see you haven't outgrown that."

"What?"

"Blushing."

"Was I supposed to outgrow it?"

He smiled. "I have no complaints. In fact I've always enjoyed watching you blush."

She tried to give him a small smile, but in all honesty, she had very little to smile about right now.

"I didn't ask if you wanted a cup of coffee. Since you didn't order a cup at that diner earlier tonight, I figured you're still not a coffee drinker."

She nodded. "And I see that you still are."

"Yep."

She frowned and broke eye contact with him to look at the cup he held in his hand. "Too much caffeine isn't good for you."

He chuckled. "So you've always said."

"And so I know. Especially now that I've become a biochemist. It's not good for your body."

Why had she said that? And why after saying it did her gaze automatically move up and down his solid frame? Bane Westmoreland was so overwhelmingly sexy. He'd always possessed a magnetism that could draw her in. The man was such a perfect hunk of carved mahogany, it was a crying shame.

She moved her gaze off his body and up to his face, thinking his facial hair gave him a sexier look. He gave her a roguish smile and she could feel her cheeks flush. "Looking at me like that can get you in a lot of trouble, Crystal Gayle," he murmured in a deep husky voice.

He was standing close, so close she could inhale his scent. Manly. Deliciously provocative. "Then, I won't look at you," she said, cutting her eyes elsewhere. Namely to her bed and all the cards and letters she'd pulled out of the satchel. "I don't need any more trouble than I'm already in. It's pretty bad when you have the government burning down your house. I'd like to see how they explain their actions to the insurance company."

"They won't have to. They will handle it in a way that makes it look like an electrical fire or something. It definitely won't appear intentional."

She lifted her chin. "Still, I don't like it." She eased up out of the chair, assuming he would step back and give her space. He didn't, and it brought their bodies within touching distance of each other.

"You look good in your T-shirt and sweats, by the way," he said softly. They were standing so close the heat of his words seemed to fan across her face.

She looked down at herself, thinking he had to be kidding. Both garments were old and ratty looking, but she remembered her manners and glanced up and said, "Thank you."

The moment she looked into his face, she wished she hadn't. The intense desire in the hazel eyes staring back at her was so profoundly sensual she felt a tug in the middle of her stomach.

Setting his coffee cup down, he moved closer. Before she knew what he was doing he reached out and placed his hands at her waist. But he didn't stop there. As he inched his hands upward and gently caressed the curve of her body, he said, "I can't get used to these. Where did all these curves come from?"

She shrugged. "Wish I knew. I just woke up one morning and they were there." Why wasn't she telling him to keep his hands to himself? Why did his touch feel so good?

He chuckled. "Only you would think these curves were an overnight thing."

Although a part of her wished he didn't do that, she kind of liked the way he would subtly remind her that they had a past. And she needed that because at times he seemed like such a stranger to her.

"Well," she said, making a move to scoot around him. But he held tight to her waist and when he began lowering his head, she could just imagine how their tongues would mingle.

The moment he took hold of her mouth, his lips ground against hers and she was powerless to do anything but kiss him back.

Bane loved kissing Crystal. Always had and figured he always would. Their kisses weren't just hot, they were flaming red-hot, and in no time he was shivering with desire. And like in the past, he had to taper his lust; otherwise he would have her spread out on that bed in no time. And he doubted she was ready for that just yet.

So he enjoyed this. The way she was provocatively returning his kiss. The way his mouth seemed to be in sync with hers, feeding off hers with a hunger he felt in every part of his body. As when he'd kissed her earlier tonight, it felt as if he'd finally come home to the woman he loved. He had been hungry for her taste for five years. He'd tried to remember just how delicious it was and knew his memories hadn't come close. The intensity was clouding his mind and he could tell she wasn't holding back, pouring everything into the kiss like he was doing.

She suddenly pulled her mouth away and drew in a deep breath. When she licked her bottom lip, he was tempted to kiss her again, take his own tongue and lick her lips.

"We should not have done that, Bane," she said softly. And the look of distress in her eyes touched him.

"Don't see why not. You're my wife."

"I don't feel like your wife."

"That can be remedied, sweetheart," he said in a provocative drawl.

"I know," she said, looking at him with a serious expression. "But sleeping with you won't make me feel as if I know you any better. I need time, Bane. I don't need you to rush me into anything."

"I won't."

She crossed her arms over her chest and he wished she hadn't done that when he saw her nipples pressed against her T-shirt. "Then, what was that kiss about just now?"

He smiled. "Passion. You can't deny you felt it. I want you so much, Crystal." He saw uneasiness line her pupils. "Relax, baby. You will let me know when you're ready. One day you will realize that no matter how long it's been, I'm still your husband."

She shook her head. "But we haven't seen each other in five years."

He frowned. Was she saying that because she wasn't sure she still loved him after all this time? He refused to believe that. "Trust me, Crystal," he heard himself say softly. "After reading all my cards and letters to you, I have no doubt you'll see what I mean."

His cell phone rang and when he turned to pick it up, she used that time to quickly move away from him and back to the bed.

"This is Bane." He nodded a few times. "Okay, Flip. Thanks and I owe you." He then clicked off the phone.

He looked over at her. "That was Flip. He wanted to let me know he collected all the items you wanted saved. And by the way. Did you know your house was bugged?"

* * *

Crystal was experiencing one shock after another. First Bane returned after five years. Then she was on the run from men who wanted to kidnap her. Then the government wanted to burn her house down. And now she was being told it was bugged?

"That's not possible. Nobody I work with has ever been invited to my home. They consider me a recluse."

Bane nodded. "Where did the stuffed giraffe come from?"

She frowned. "The stuffed giraffe?"

"Yes."

She thought for a minute. "It was a gift from one of my coworkers, who took a trip to South Africa earlier this year. She brought everyone souvenirs back."

"Who was this generous person?"

"A biochemist by the name of Jasmine Ross."

"Well, yours was given to you with a purpose. Flip saw it on your dresser and figured it would be something you'd want to keep, as well. When his sensor went off he knew it contained an audio bugging device. He proved his suspicions true when he gutted it. I guess someone thought they could catch you saying something about your research on the phone or something."

"Well, they were wrong." Things were getting crazier by the minute and she couldn't believe it. "Were there others?"

Bane shook his head. "Flip and his brothers combed the rest of the house and didn't detect anything. Now you see why Homeland Security wants to burn it down to the ground?"

No, she still didn't see it. "They could have found another way."

"Evidently not."

She didn't like Bane's attitude, as if he was perfectly fine with someone torching the place where she lived. Turning her back to him, she angrily began shoving all the cards and envelopes back into the satchel. She was in no mood to read anything now. All she wanted to do was get into bed and rest her brain.

"I'll take my shower now."

"Fine." Crystal was tempted to turn around but refused to do so. She planned to be in bed and dead asleep by the time he came out of the bathroom.

When she heard the bathroom door close she released a deep sigh. How were she and Bane going to share a hotel room without…

She shook her head. The thought of them making love was driving her nuts. All of a sudden the memories of their last time together were taking hold of her. They had been happy. They had just gotten married and thought the future was theirs to grab and keep.

When she heard the water from his shower she couldn't help but recall when they had showered together. All the things he had taught her to do. Bane had been the best teacher, and he'd always been easy and gentle with her.

As she drew the bedcovers back and then slid beneath them, she tried to not think of Bane. Instead, she thought of her house and how at that very minute it could be going up in flames.

Eleven

Twenty minutes later Bane walked out of the bathroom and glanced over at the bed where Crystal lay sleeping. Or was she? He found it amusing that she was pretending to be asleep while checking out his bare chest and the way his sweats rode low on his hips. He had no problem with her ogling him; she could even touch him if she liked. Better yet, he would love for her to invite him to her bed. He would love to slide between the sheets with her.

Intending to give her more to look at, he decided he might as well get on the floor and do his daily exercises. He'd begin with push-ups after a five-minute flex routine that included bending to touch his toes. Maybe a vigorous workout would work out all the desire that was overtaking his senses and at the same time arouse her enough that she would want him to make love to her. It was worth a try.

Less than thirty minutes into his exercises he wondered if she realized her breathing had changed. He most certainly had noticed. Now he was off the floor and running in place. His sweats had ridden even lower on his hips and his bare chest was wet from sweat. Now for a few crunches.

"What you're doing doesn't make sense, Bane."

He forced himself not to smile. "I thought you were asleep," he said, lying, when he knew she'd been peeking through a slightly closed eye at him.

"How could I sleep with all that racket you're making down there on the floor?"

"Sorry if I disturbed you. And what doesn't make sense?"

"For a person to take a shower only to get all sweaty again."

He chuckled. "I'll take another shower. No problem."

She had shifted in bed to lie on her side and look over at him. "You did three hundred push-ups. Who does that?"

"A SEAL who needs to stay in shape." Evidently she'd been counting right along with him but had missed a few. "And I did three hundred and twenty-five." He wondered where her concentration had been when he'd done the other twenty-five.

"Whatever. I just hope that's the last of it."

"For tonight. I do the same thing each morning. But I'll try to be a little quieter so as not to disturb you."

The sound of him exercising wasn't what was disturbing her, Crystal thought, trying not to let her gaze roam all over Bane. Jeez. How could sweat look so good on a man? It was such a turn-on. All that testosterone being worked up like that. Rippling muscles. Bulging biceps. Firm abs. Mercy! She'd gone without sex for five years and it had never bothered her before. But now it did. Only because the man here with her now was Bane.

She had pretended to be asleep when he'd come out of the bathroom. But seeing him bare chested and wearing sweats was just too much. She had tried closing her eyes and holding them shut. Tight. But the sounds of him grunting sent all kinds of fantasies through her mind and she'd begun peeking. And definitely getting an eyeful. If she didn't know better she'd think he'd deliberately gone after her attention.

"I've worked up an appetite. Do you want something?"

She had worked up an appetite watching him as well, but it wasn't for food. She definitely wanted something, but it was something she'd best do without—it was just too soon since Bane had come for her, and she needed to stay focused until she was out of danger. "No thanks. I'm still full from those waffles and chicken we ate earlier. But you can order room service if you like. The hotel clerk did say the kitchen was open twenty-four hours." But who wanted to eat at four in the morning?

He glanced at the clock on the nightstand separating the beds. "I think I'll order something up. Nothing heavy. If I do it now, it will probably arrive by the time I get out of the shower. But if they come while I'm in the shower, don't open the door for anyone. They can wait a few minutes. If they can't, then they can take it back to the kitchen."

She wondered if all that was necessary. But then all she had to remember was her house was probably getting burned to the ground about now. "Fine." She hoped by the time he got out of the shower for a second time that night she would be asleep for real. But that hadn't worked during his first shower—the sound of running water and picturing him naked beneath that water had kept her awake.

She watched as he moved over to the desk and picked up the phone to order a steak dinner with potatoes. At four in the morning? She lifted a brow. Hadn't he said nothing heavy? If that wasn't heavy then what was his definition?

And speaking of heavy…

Why had her breathing suddenly gone that way? Could it be because her gaze had now landed on the perspiration dripping off his hard chest, past those chiseled muscles, and making a path toward the waistband of his sweats? And why did the thought of licking it before the drops of sweat could disappear beneath the waistband actually appeal to her?

He had grabbed more clothes and was about to go into the bathroom when his cell phone rang. "That's Nick," Bane said, turning and heading back toward the desk.

Crystal felt a tightening of her stomach. It seemed that whenever this guy Nick called, he was the bearer of bad news. "Maybe they changed their minds about burning down my house."

The look Bane gave her all but said not to count on it. "Yes, Nick?"

She saw the tightening of Bane's jaw and the dark and stormy look in his eyes. And when he said, "Damn" three times she felt uneasy and suspected the news wasn't good.

"Thanks for letting me know. We're on the road again. Contact Viper. He'll know what to do."

Crystal had eased up on the side of the bed. As soon

as he clicked off the phone she was about to ask what was wrong when he asked, "Where's your jacket?"

She lifted a brow. "My jacket?"

"Yes."

"Hanging up in the closet. Why?"

"It has a tracking device on it."

"What!"

Already Bane had reached the closet and jerked her jacket off the hanger. She watched in horror as he took a pocketknife and ripped through a seam. "Bingo." He pulled out a small item that looked like a gold button.

She drew in a deep breath and met Bane's gaze when he looked over at her. "Does that mean…"

"Yes. Someone has been keeping up with our whereabouts all this time, and chances are they know we're here."

"But how did someone get my jacket?"

"Probably at work. Do you keep it on during the day?"

"No. I always take it off, hang it up and put on my lab coat."

He nodded. "Then, you have your answer. And I suspect the person who put this tracker in your coat is the same person who gave you the stuffed giraffe." He rubbed his hands down his face. "Come on. Let's pack up and get the hell out of here."

"But what about your food? Your shower?"

"I'll stop somewhere later to grab something, but for now we need to put as much distance between us and this place as we can. As for my shower, you'll just have to put up with sharing a car with a musky man."

"I can handle it." She was already on her feet and pulling out her luggage. She considered how Bane hadn't expected all this drama when he'd come looking for her. "I'm sorry, Bane." She glanced over at him and saw he was doing likewise with his luggage.

He paused in tossing items into his duffel bag and looked back at her. "For what?"

"For being the cause of so much trouble. I guess you hadn't figured on all of this."

"No, but it doesn't matter, Crystal. You're my wife, and I will protect you with my life if it came to that."

She shivered at the thought and hoped it didn't. But still, the words he'd just spoken had a profound impact on her. She pushed several locks of hair back from her face to focus on Bane as he continued to pack. Surprisingly, it wasn't Bane's sexiness that was wearing her down, but his ability to still want her in spite of everything.

"Ready?"

She nodded. "Yes."

"We need to be aware of our surroundings more than ever and make sure we aren't being tailed. There's a pretty good chance someone is sitting and waiting for us in the parking lot, which is why I'm putting plan B in place."

"What's plan B?"

"You'll see."

After Bane checked up and down the hallway, they left the hotel room, moving quickly toward the stairwell instead of the elevator. She followed his lead and didn't ask any questions. And when they came to a locked door that led to the courtyard, he used what looked like a knitting needle to pick the lock.

"Still doing that, I see," she said.

He shrugged. "Not as much as I used to."

In no time the lock gave way and she saw they were in the courtyard, which was located on the other side of the building from the parking lot. "How will we get to our car?"

"We won't."

She was about to ask what he meant when suddenly a white SUV pulled up, tailed by a dark sedan. Since Bane didn't seemed alarmed by the two vehicles, she figured he knew the occupants. When the door to the SUV opened and a big bruiser of a man got out, she saw Bane's lips ease into a smile.

When the man came to a stop in front of them, Bane said. "Crystal, I want you to meet Gavin Blake, better known as Viper. Another one of my teammates."

Bane wasn't bothered by the way Viper was checking out Crystal. He was curious, as most of his teammates were. They had wondered what kind of woman could keep a man faithful to a wife he hadn't seen in five years. Bane could tell that Viper, a known ladies' man, was in awe, if his stare was anything to go by.

Moments later, Viper switched his intense gaze from Crystal back to Bane. "She's beautiful, Bane."

"You forgot to check out my teeth," Crystal said, frowning.

Viper let out a deep laugh. "And she has a good sense of humor," he added. "I like that. She's definitely a keeper."

"Yes, she is." Bane had known that the first day he'd met Crystal. "Did you check out the parking lot?"

Viper nodded. "Yes, and it was just like you figured. A car with two men inside is parked beside the one you were driving. I phoned in the description and the license plates to Nick, and according to him, it's the same vehicle an eyewitness saw in the area when one of the other biochemists was kidnapped. So you did the right thing by having Nick call me."

Viper nodded toward the SUV. "Here's your new ride. Chances are those guys don't know you're onto them. They probably planned to snatch your wife the minute you checked out of the hotel tomorrow morning."

"Like hell."

"That's what I said," Viper said, chuckling. "I figured they don't have a clue who they're messing with. I'm going to keep those guys busy while you and your lady get a head start. This ought to be fun."

Bane frowned. "Don't enjoy yourself too much."

"I won't. I brought my marine cousin with me to make sure I stay out of trouble. At least as much as I can," Viper said, handing Bane the keys to the SUV. "Do you have a plan from here?"

Bane nodded. "Yes. My brother is calling in family members with connections to law enforcement."

Viper nodded. "That's good. There's nothing like family backing you when you're in a pinch." He then turned his attention back to Crystal and smiled. "It was nice finally getting to meet you. You have a good man here. And, Bane, if you need my help again, just call." With those words, Viper walked away and got inside the dark sedan before the driver pulled off.

Bane watched him leave before turning his attention to Crystal. "Come on, let's get the hell out of here before those guys sitting in the parking lot figure out we're one up on them." He opened the trunk and placed their luggage inside.

"Do you want me to drive, Bane? You have to be tired."

He smiled when he opened the SUV's door for her to

get in. What he was enduring was nothing compared to missions he and his teammates typically encountered. "No, I'm fine. We're together, and that's all that matters to me."

We're together, and that's all that matters to me.

A half hour later, as Bane took the interstate with a remarkable amount of ease for a man who hadn't gotten much rest, Crystal couldn't help but continue to recall those words. Shouldn't that be all that mattered to her, as well? The one thing she knew for certain was that she was glad he was here with her. No telling what her fate would be if he wasn't. She wouldn't have known where to go or what to do. Her plans had been to head for the Bahamas, not knowing someone would have been there, waiting for her at the airport to grab her before she could get on the plane.

But Bane had known. Through his intricate network of teammates, he'd been able to stay one step ahead of the bad guys. What had gone down at the hotel was too close for comfort. She would never have known a tracker had been sewn inside her jacket.

She was surprised Jasmine Ross was involved. The woman was a few years older than she and seemed perky enough. Jasmine had even tried to befriend her a few times, but Crystal hadn't been ready to become the woman's friend. She hadn't thought anything about the stuffed giraffe, since Jasmine had given everyone working in the lab a gift. And as for her jacket, Crystal hung it on the coatrack like everyone else, so Jasmine had access to it. She could have sneaked off with it and placed a tracker inside without being detected.

Crystal wondered what would entice a person to be on the wrong side of the law. What was in it for the

woman? Crystal didn't want to think about what those
other two chemists were enduring against their will.
They'd been separated from their families and probably didn't know if anyone would find and rescue them.
Were they even still in this country?

"You okay over there?"

She glanced at Bane. As far as she was concerned,
she should be asking him that. At least she'd gotten a
couple hours of sleep earlier tonight. "Yes, I'm fine.
What about you?"

He chuckled. "I'm great."

To a degree, she believed him. Bane was definitely
in his element. This was a different Bane. More in control. Disciplined. Not impulsive, irresponsible or reck-
less. The Bane she remembered would have gone out
to the parking lot to confront those guys, ready to kick
ass. The old Bane had an attitude and detested anyone
telling him what to do, especially when it involved her.
That was why he'd butted heads with her father countless times and defied the law.

And defied his family. She recalled how often his
brother Dillon had sat them down and talked to them,
urging her to stay in school. He had lectured them to
stop acting impulsively and to start thinking of someone other than themselves.

Deciding to continue the conversation with the goal
of keeping him awake, she asked, "So what's going on
with your family? Are your brothers and cousins still
single?"

His laugh was rich and filled the car's interior. The
sound filled her as well, and she wondered how the
deep throatiness of his voice could do that to her. "Not
hardly. In fact, after Valentine's Day when Bailey ties
the knot, that will take care of everyone."

"Bailey is getting married?"

"Yes, and she's moving to Alaska. Her husband-to-be owns a huge spread on an island there."

Crystal was shocked. "Bailey always swore that she would never marry and move away."

"Well, evidently Walker Rafferty was able to change her mind about that. I got a chance to meet him over Thanksgiving. A pretty nice guy. Ex-marine."

The man must really be something if Bane approved of him. As the youngest two Westmorelands, Bane and Bailey had been close growing up. They'd done a lot of things together. Even got into trouble. "I'm happy for her."

"So am I."

She then listened as he brought her up-to-date on his other siblings and cousins and the women and men they had married. His cousins Zane and Derringer, and his brother Riley were also shockers. She remembered they had reputations around Denver as being ladies' men.

She shifted to get comfortable in her seat as Bane continued to fill her in on his family. She loved hearing the sound of his voice and could tell he was proud of everyone in the Westmoreland family. He also told her about more cousins his family had tracked down in Alaska with the last name of Outlaw.

As she continued to listen to him, she didn't think to question where they were headed. Like he'd said earlier, they were together, and that was all that mattered. She felt safe with him, and at the moment she couldn't imagine being anyplace else.

Twelve

"I'm taking the bed closer to the door again."

"All right."

Bane tossed his duffel bag on the bed and glanced around the hotel room. This one was roomier than the last and the bed looked inviting as hell. The first thing he intended to do was take a shower. He had driven for nine hours and he had to hand it to Crystal, she had tried keeping him company by engaging him in conversation about his family and his job as a SEAL. He had explained that due to the highly classified nature of what he did, there was a lot about his missions he couldn't divulge. She understood and seemed fascinated by what he had been able to tell her.

He glanced over at her and could tell she was exhausted, as well. It was daylight outside but he figured as long as they kept the curtains drawn the room would have the effect of nighttime. Right now he doubted his body cared that it was just two in the afternoon. As long as he could get a little sleep, he would be ready for the next phase of his mission to keep his wife safe.

He turned to place his cell phone on the nightstand. He'd received text messages from Flip letting them know Crystal's house had been burned down to the ground, which probably infuriated those thinking she had data stored somewhere inside it. And then Viper had texted to say that before turning those guys in the parking lot over to Homeland Security, he and his cousin had given them something to think about. Bane hadn't asked for details, thinking it was best not to know. But he figured the men wanting Crystal had to be insanely mad when their plans were derailed time and time again. Hopefully, if those guys were the same ones who had kidnapped the other two chemists, it would be just a matter of time before they were found.

"Do you want me to order you something to eat? That way when you get out of the shower your food will be here," Crystal asked.

He glanced back over at her. "That would be nice. Thanks."

"Anything in particular you want?"

It was close to the tip of his tongue to answer and say, *Yes, you. You are what I want.* Instead, he said, "Whatever looks good. I'm game." Grabbing some fresh clothes out of the duffel bag, he went into the bathroom and closed the door behind him. And then he leaned against it and drew in a deep breath.

Needing a shower was just an excuse. What he really needed was breathing space away from Crystal. Sharing a room with her, being in close proximity to her after all this time was playing havoc on every part of his body. Every time he looked at her he was filled with desire

so deep, the essence of it seemed to drench his pores.
And he couldn't ignore the sensations he felt knowing
they were finally together after being apart for so long.

The sound of his phone alerted him to a text message
from Nick. Pulling the phone out of his back pocket, he
quickly read the lengthy text before placing his phone
on the vanity.

Stripping off his clothes, he stepped into the shower.
A cold one. And he didn't so much as flinch when
the icy cold water bore down on his skin. Instead, he
growled, sounding like a male calling out for a mate he
wanted but couldn't have.

Deciding to focus on something else to get his mind
off Crystal for the time being, he mentally ran through
all the information Nick had texted him. Crystal's co-
worker, Jasmine Ross, was nowhere to be found. Rumor
within Homeland Security indicated she'd had help from
inside, and for that reason Nick agreed with Bane's way
of thinking to not let anyone, especially Homeland Security, know of his connection to Crystal. Right now
everyone was trying to figure out where she'd gone.

The plan was for him and Crystal to stay put at this
hotel until tomorrow. Then they would drive overnight
to the Alabama and Georgia line and meet with some of
his family members. Namely his cousins Dare, Quade,
Cole and Clint Westmoreland. Dare, a former FBI agent,
was currently sheriff of College Park, a suburb of Atlanta. Clint and Cole were former Texas Rangers and
Quade still dabbled from time to time in secretive as-
signments for a branch of government connected directly to the White House.

Bane stepped out of the shower and began towel-
ing himself off, ready to have something to eat and
then finally get some sleep. After slipping into a pair

of jeans and a T-shirt, he grabbed his phone and slid it into his back pocket. He then opened the bathroom door and walked out to find Crystal pacing the hotel room. "What's wrong?"

She paused and looked over her shoulder at him. "What makes you think something is wrong?"

"You're pacing."

"So I was." She moved to the desk and sat down in the black leather armchair. "Too much nervous energy, I guess. I don't want to bother you."

"You aren't bothering me," he said, moving to his duffel bag to discard the clothes he'd just taken off. "I just don't want you to wear yourself out."

"You're worried about me wearing myself out? You? Who barely got any sleep or ate a decent meal in the past twenty-four hours?"

"I've survived before on less."

"Well, I prefer not hearing about it."

He wondered if she was ready to hear what Nick had texted him earlier. "Jasmine Ross is missing."

"Missing?"

"Yes. Nick thinks she might have suspected DHS is onto her and went into hiding." At that moment there was a knock on the door, followed by a voice that said, "Room service."

"Great timing," Bane said as he headed for the door. Deciding not to take any chances, he grabbed his gun off the table and then looked through the peephole before opening the door.

After the attendant had rolled in a cart loaded down with a variety of foods, arranged everything and left, Bane smiled over at Crystal. "The food looks good. You're joining me, right?"

She nodded. "Yes, I'm joining you."

* * *

"I doubt if I can eat another bite, Bane," Crystal said, sliding her chair back from the table. Her goal had been to make sure he got something to eat and not the other way around. But he'd had other ideas and had practically fed her off his plate. She recalled how they used to do stuff like that years ago. Until now, she hadn't realized just how intimate it was.

"Mmm, you've got to try this. The piecrust is so flaky it nearly melts in your mouth," he said, reaching over and offering her his fork with a portion of apple pie on it.

It slid easily between her lips and she closed her eyes and moaned. He was right. It was delicious. In fact, everything was. Instead of ordering an entrée, she had chosen a variety of appetizers she thought he might like. And from the way he'd dived in, he had been pretty hungry. She was glad he had enjoyed all her selections.

She watched him finish off the last of the pie and tried ignoring the way her own stomach fluttered. He even looked sexy while he ate. Seriously, how totally ridiculous was that? Sighing, she glanced around the hotel room, deciding she could handle looking at just about anything right now except Bane. More than once she'd noticed him looking at her and had recognized that glint in his eyes. He'd always had that look when he wanted her. And why was she having such a hard time getting past that look?

"It's hard to believe the sun is about to go down already."

She glanced over at him and saw he was looking out the window. She had opened the blinds while he was taking a shower so the room wouldn't look so dark. The light coming through the window had helped, but now they would be losing that daylight soon.

"We'll make the twenty-four-hour mark in a few hours."

She lifted a brow. "Twenty-four-hour mark?"

He smiled and stared at her for what seemed like a minute or two before saying, "We will have spent the past twenty-four hours together. That's a pretty good start, don't you think?"

Pretty good start? Considering everything, he could think that? "I suppose." She glanced at her watch. "Now it's my turn to shower. I plan on getting into bed early."

"So do I."

She glanced at him and saw gorgeous hazel eyes staring back at her across the rim of a coffee cup. She couldn't help but return his stare. Okay, what was going on here and why was she encouraging it? He shouldn't be looking at her like that and she certainly shouldn't be returning the look. She should be saying something… or better yet, shouldn't she be getting up from her chair and heading for the bathroom? Yes, that was exactly what she should be doing.

She cleared her throat before easing to her feet. And because she felt she needed to say something she said, "Umm, I think I'll take a tub bath instead of a shower. I feel the need to soak my body in bubbles for a while." She frowned. Seriously? Wasn't that too much information?

She knew it probably had been when she saw his smile. It wasn't just any old smile but one that was so sexy it had sparks of desire shooting all through her.

"Sounds nice. Mind if I join you?"

Why had he had to ask her that? And why had his gaze just lowered to her chest just now? And why were her nipples stiffening into buds and feeling achy against her T-shirt? "You took a shower earlier. Besides, you'd be bored to tears."

His rich chuckle filled the room. "Bored to tears? In a bathtub with you? I seriously doubt that, sweetheart. In fact, I know for sure that won't be the case."

She raked her eyes over him from head to toe. She had a feeling that wouldn't be the case as well, but would never confess that to him. "But I'm sure such a macho SEAL wouldn't want to smell like vanilla," she said, moving quickly to the bed where she'd laid out a change of clothes.

Grabbing the items off the bed, she dashed into the bathroom and closed the door behind her.

Bane took the last sip of his coffee as he continued to stare at the closed door. Did he have his wife running scared? He grinned, thinking how he'd at least asked about taking a bath with her…even if she'd turned him down. Already he heard the sound of running water and his mind was beginning to work overtime, conjuring up all kinds of fantasy scenarios involving Crystal's naked body and a bathtub full of bubbles.

He had it bad. Yes, he most certainly did. But hell, that could be expected. He was a full-grown man who hadn't shared a woman's bed in five years, and the woman he'd been holding out for was behind that closed door without a stitch of clothes on, playing with bubbles and smelling like vanilla.

He shifted his gaze from the closed door to glance out the window. He might as well get up and close the blinds, since it was getting dark outside. However, instead of moving, he continued to gaze thoughtfully out of the window. He wondered how long it would be before he could officially bring Crystal out of hiding. According to Nick's text messages, two arrests had been made, but so far those guys weren't talking.

Just then, his phone went off. He picked it up when he recognized the ringtone. "Yes, Bay?"

"Just checking on you and Crystal. Dillon told us what's going on."

Bane leaned back in his chair. "So far so good, considering someone had sewn a tracker inside Crystal's jacket. Luckily, we were able to stay ahead of them anyway."

"Dillon said you're headed south. Why not come home to Westmoreland Country?"

"Can't do that. The last thing the family needs is for me to deliver trouble to everyone's doorstep."

"We can handle it, Bane."

"It's not the old days, Bay. My brothers and cousins have wives and kids now. We're dealing with a bunch of crazies and there's no telling what they might do. I can't take the chance."

"Then, come to Kodiak. Walker told me to tell you that you and Crystal are welcome there. We're leaving for home tomorrow and won't be returning to Westmoreland Country until a week before Christmas."

Bane smiled. "Did you hear what you just said?"

"About what?"

"Kodiak, Alaska. You said that you and Walker were leaving for *home* tomorrow. It's strange hearing you think of anywhere other than Denver as home."

Bailey chuckled. "I guess I'm beginning to think of wherever Walker is as home for me."

Bane nodded. "You really love the guy, don't you?"

"Yes. Now I know how you and Crystal felt all those years ago. Especially the obsession. I can't imagine my life without Walker." She paused a moment and then asked, "And how are things going with you and Crystal? You guys still love each other, right?"

"Why wouldn't we?"

"The two of you haven't seen each other in five years, Bane. That's a long time to not have any kind of communication with someone."

Yes, it was, but he'd known the moment he'd seen Crystal that for him nothing had changed. But could he say the same about her feelings for him?

Before his cousin could ask him any more sensitive questions, he said, "I need to make a call, Bay. Thank Walker for the offer and tell him if I decide to take him up on it, I'll let him know."

"Okay. Stay safe and continue to keep Crystal safe."

"I can't handle my business any other way."

He ended the call, then stood and closed the blinds before wheeling the table and dishes out into the hall. Once back inside he reached for his phone, figuring now was a good time to check in with Nick before calling it a night. His friend picked up on the second ring. "What's going on, Nick?"

"Glad you called. I was about to text you. Jasmine Ross has been found."

Crystal drew in a deep breath as she slid into her bathrobe. She felt good and refreshed. Soaking in the tub for almost an hour had definitely relaxed her mind. Hopefully Bane was asleep by now and she would be soon, too. They both needed a good ten hours' worth before heading out again.

Opening the bathroom door she allowed her eyes to adjust to the semidarkness. The first thing she noticed was that Bane was not in bed sleeping as she had hoped but was sitting at the desk with his back to her.

He turned around when he heard her and she could tell from the look on his face that something was wrong.

"Bane? What's going on?"

He stood and stuck his hands into the pockets of his jeans. "I talked to Nick a short while ago."

Nick, who was usually the bearer of bad news, she thought, tightening the belt of her robe around her. "And?"

"They found Jasmine Ross."

"Really?" she said, moving toward Bane with a feeling of excitement flowing through her. "That's good news, right? Hopefully Jasmine will confess her part in all this and work out a plea deal or something. Maybe they'll get her to tell them where those other two chemists are being held."

"Unfortunately, Jasmine won't be telling anyone anything."

Crystal frowned. "Why?"

"Because she's dead. She was shot in the head and dumped in a lake. A couple of fishermen came across her body a few hours ago."

Thirteen

"Here. Drink this."

Crystal's fingers tightened on the glass Bane placed in her hand, and she fought hard to hold it steady. Jasmine was dead? Suddenly everything seemed so unreal. So unbelievable.

She glanced down into the liquid. It was alcohol, and the smell alone was so strong it had her straightening up a little in her chair. "Whoa. What is it?"

"Scotch."

She lifted an arched brow. "Where did Scotch come from?"

"I ordered it from room service after I talked with Nick. I figured you'd need a glass."

"I don't drink, Bane."

"You need to drink this. It will help with the shock of what I told you."

Crystal nodded, took a sip and frowned. Like coffee, liquor was a taste she'd never acquired. She drew in a deep breath as her gaze flickered around the room.

"She brought it on herself, Crystal," she heard Bane say. "Evidently, the woman didn't have any problem setting you up. Don't forget she placed a bugging device in a gift she gave you and a tracker inside your jacket."

"I know, but it's still hard to believe she'd do something like that. She was nice most of the time. At least she pretended to be," Crystal said, leaning forward to place her glass on the desk. One sip had been enough for her. "How could she have gotten mixed up in something so devious?"

Bane shrugged. "Who knows what makes people do what they do? Unfortunately, she got in too far over her head. And the people she thought she could trust saw her as a threat instead of an asset."

Shivers passed through Crystal, and when Bane touched her arm she nearly jumped out of her skin. "You okay?" he asked softly.

She tipped her head all the way back to gaze up at the ceiling before lowering it to look at him. "Not really. It was bad enough to know one of my coworkers was involved in heaven knows what, but then to find out she lost her life because of it is a little too much."

"Are you sure you're okay?"

She glanced at Bane. "Yes, pretty much. But I think I'll go to bed now and try to get some sleep."

Crystal stood up. Without saying anything else and feeling Jasmine's death weighing her down, she moved across the room, threw back the covers and slid into bed. She turned her back to Bane so he wouldn't be able to see her tears.

Bane came awake with a start. First there was a small whimper from the bed next to his. Then he heard a rumbled, emotional plea. "Please don't! Don't shoot him. Please don't."

It took only a second to realize Crystal was thrashing around in her bed having a bad dream. He was out of his bed in a flash and flipped on the small lamp on the nightstand, bathing the room in a soft glow. He sat on the edge of her bed, gently shaking her awake. "Crystal, it's okay. Wake up, baby. You're having a bad dream. Wake up."

He watched as her eyes flew open just seconds before she threw herself into his arms. Automatically he held her tight and used his hands to gently stroke her back. "It's okay, Crystal."

"Bane."

She whispered his name against his neck and the heat from her breath set off a fire in the pit of his stomach. Her arms tightened around him and he refused to let this moment pass. She needed him and he wanted to be needed.

"I'm here, baby."

She pulled back slowly, meeting his gaze and holding it. "It was an awful dream. They came for us, and you wouldn't let them take me. You put yourself in front of me. To protect me. And the man raised his gun to shoot. They were going to shoot you and I felt so helpless."

He slid one hand to the back of her neck and used the other to push several strands of hair back from her face. He saw fear in her eyes, and more than anything he wanted to take that look away. "It was just a dream, Crystal. No one is here but us, and no one is going to shoot me."

"B-but I…"

"Shh, baby. It's okay. I'm okay. We're okay."

He leaned in close to kiss the corners of her lips but

she tipped her head at an angle and his mouth landed over hers. Instinctively, she parted her lips at the moment of impact and he swept his tongue inside her mouth to kiss her fully.

They'd kissed a couple of times over the past twenty-four hours, but nothing like this. There had been a hunger, but tonight this was about taking care of an ache. He deepened the kiss to taste her more fully as desire quickened inside him. She whimpered, and the sound was so unlike the one that had awakened him earlier. This one sent sensations jolting through him, filling him with the awareness of a sexual need that he felt all over.

And when she reached up and wrapped her arms around his neck it became the kind of kiss that curled a man's toes and made his entire body get hard. She tangled her tongue with his in a way that made every cell in his body come alive and he could only moan out loud.

A swirl of heat combined with a heavy dose of want overtook him as he continued to ply her mouth with hungry, languorous strokes of his tongue. There was only so much of her he could take without craving more, and his desire for more was nearly eating him alive, driving him insane.

And he didn't want to just kiss her. He wanted to make love to her the way a husband would want to make love to his wife. He wanted to taste her all over. Feel his hands touching every inch of her. And reacquaint himself with being inside her.

Exploring her mouth this way was making his already aroused body that much more unrestrained. It was hard to remain in his good-guy lane and stay in control. Especially when she was returning his kiss with just as much bone-melting fire as he was putting into it. Explosive chemistry was something they'd always shared. Nothing had changed. The taste of her was incredibly pleasurable as always. To his way of thinking, even more so.

Unable to take any more, he broke off the kiss and pressed his forehead to hers while releasing pent-up breath from deep in his lungs. "Crystal." He wasn't sure why he needed to whisper her name at that particular moment, but he did.

"I'm here, Bane."

Yes, she most certainly was, he thought, breathing hard. He briefly considered giving her another kiss before tucking her under the covers and returning to his bed, but for some reason he couldn't do that. He wanted to continue holding her in his arms, so she would know she was safe here with him.

Bane shifted their bodies so they were stretched out together in the bed, and as they lay there beside each other, he wrapped his arms around her. "Sleep now," he whispered softly, trying to ignore how the angle of her backside was smacked up against his groin. He had a hard-on and there was no way she couldn't feel it.

She began writhing around in the bed trying to get comfortable, and each time she did so he felt his engorged erection get that much harder. Finally, after gritting his teeth a few times, he reached out and cupped a firm hold to her thigh. "I wouldn't do that too often if I were you," he warned.

"Why? Because you want me?"

With a guttural hiss, he positioned her body so that she was lying flat on her back. He loomed over her and looked down into her eyes. "What do you think?"

She broke eye contact with him for a mere second before returning his gaze. "I think I might not be as good with that as I used to be."

"Why would you think that?"

"It's been a while. Five years."

A smile curved his lips. "Are you saying that because you think that I might not be as good as I used to be, as well?"

Surprise leaped into her eyes and she exhaled sharply. "No. That never crossed my mind."

"Good. And just for the record, the thought that you're not as good as you used to be never crossed mine, either."

"Not even once?"

He stared at her in the lamplight. Her features were beautiful, the look in her eyes intense as she waited on his answer. "Not even once," he said, meaning every word. "But I have been wondering about something, though," he added, breathing her scent deep into his nostrils.

She lifted a brow. "What?"

"Can my tongue still make you come?"

Bane's words caused Crystal to squeeze her eyes shut as sensations, namely memories of him doing that very thing, assailed her. She always thought Bane's mouth should be outlawed. And it didn't take much to recall everything he used to do, while licking her from the top of her head to the bottom of her feet, paying close attention to those areas in between.

Especially those areas in between.

"Open your eyes, sweetheart."

She did and her gaze met his. Held it. She felt the sexual tension mounting between them, easing them into a comfortable and mutual existence where memories were surrounding them in ways they couldn't ignore or deny. And at the exact moment his fingers shifted from her thigh to settle between her legs, she knew just what he'd found.

A woman who was hot and ready.

Crystal wasn't exactly sure when the amount of time they'd been apart no longer mattered to her. The only thing that mattered was that he still wanted her after so long. That he hadn't been with another woman just like she hadn't been with another man. It was as if her body was his and his was hers. They had known it, accepted it and endured the loneliness. She hadn't wanted any other man but him, and now her body was demanding to have what it had gone without for quite some time.

"Do you know how many times I lay in bed at night and envisioned touching you this way, Crystal?" Bane whispered.

He shifted his hand and his fingers began moving, sliding inside her, and automatically her thighs eased apart. "No, how many?" she asked, loving how the tip of his fingers stroked up and down her clit.

"Too many. Those were the times I had to take matters into my own hands. Literally. That's how I kept from going insane. But I like this better," he said as he continued working his fingers inside her, causing a deep ache to spread through her. "The real thing. No holds barred."

No holds barred. As he stroked the juncture between her thighs, Crystal couldn't recall the last time she had felt so electrified. For so long, she had mostly ignored her body's demands, except for those rare occasions when she couldn't and had resorted to self-pleasure the way he had.

But Bane's fingers were not toys. They were real, and what they were doing to her was as real as it could get. The sensations being generated inside her were so intense she actually felt air being ripped right out of her lungs with every breath she took. Her heart rate had picked up, and she felt as if she was being driven off the edge, falling headfirst into one powerful wave of pleasure.

"You like this?"

Before she could answer, he reached down, sliding his free hand beneath her shirt and settling it on the center of her stomach. She felt the heat radiating from his touch and began writhing. "Hey, it's okay, baby. It's just me and my touch. I want to put my imprint on you everywhere," he whispered.

Did he think his imprint wasn't already there? She was convinced his fingertips had burned into her skin years ago. And when he pushed her T-shirt up, she felt a whoosh of air touch her skin, especially her breasts. She wasn't wearing a bra and could feel the heat of his gaze as he stared down at the twin globes.

"Hmm, beautiful. Just as I remembered. Do you have any idea how much I used to enjoy sucking these?"

Yes, she had an idea because he used to do so all the time. At one point she'd been convinced his mouth was made just for her nipples. And now, when he used his tongue to lick his lips just moments before lowering his head toward her breasts, she could actually feel a fire ignite inside her. She felt her nipples harden even more. And all it took was one look into his eyes to know he was about to devour her alive.

He buried his face in her chest and took her nipple easily between his lips. Then he began sucking hard. She wasn't sure if it was his fingers working inside her below or his mouth torturing her nipples that would do her in first. When it happened, she had a feeling it was both.

"Bane!"

An orgasm tore through her immediately and she couldn't hold back the scream. But he was there, capturing her mouth with his, smothering her deep moans with his kiss. Still, he didn't let up, his fingers continuing to work her, rebuilding a degree of passion within her that she could not contain. And when he released her mouth, he began licking her skin from the base of her chin, all over her breasts, down past her stomach all the way to where his mouth met his fingers. He pulled his fingers out of her only to lift her hips to bring the essence of her toward his mouth. The moment his tongue slid inside her she shuddered, filled to the rim with flames of erotic desire.

She pushed on his shoulders but he wasn't letting up. It was as if he was a hungry beast who intended to get his fill, and when another orgasm ripped through her, she cried out his name again. For a fraction of a second, she was convinced she had died and gone to heaven.

But she was quickly snatched back to earth when she felt him lower her hips and remove his mouth from her. Then she watched through languid eyes as he stood and began stripping off his clothes before reaching down to practically tear off hers. A raw, primitive need was overtaking him. It stirred the air, and she could see it in the passion-glazed eyes staring down at her. She felt the heat in every part of her body.

"That was just the beginning," he whispered as he slid a condom on his engorged erection. "Just the beginning."

And then he was back, spreading her thighs, looming over her, and when their gazes met, she saw what she'd always seen when he'd made love to her. Love. Pure, unadulterated love. Bane still loved her and she knew at that moment that no matter what they'd gone through and what they were going through now, she still loved him, as well.

She reached out and slid her hands up his back, feeling the deep cords of his muscles and flinching when she came to several scars that hadn't been there before. But before she could even imagine what story those scars told, he was taking her mouth again, pulling her in and consuming her with a need that was demanding her full concentration. On them. On this. Never had she been filled with such overwhelming desire, need and passion. She wanted him. Her husband. The man who had been her first and only best friend. The man who'd always had her back and had defied anyone who'd tried keeping them apart.

He ended the kiss to stare down at her. "You ready?"

She looked up at him, dragging in a deep whoosh of air filled with their heated scents. "Yes, I'm ready."

And then, holding tight to her hips, spreading her thighs even wider, he slid inside her.

Bane pushed into Crystal all the way until he couldn't go any farther, not sure where his body began and hers ended. The only thing he knew was this was home. He was home. He had been gone five years and that was five years too long. But now he was back and intended to remind her just how good they were together. Remind her why she was his and he was hers.

His blood was boiling, and at that moment it seemed as though all of it had rushed to the head of his erection buried deep inside her. He felt compelled to move, to mate, to drown even deeper into her sweet, delicious depths. He felt her inner muscles clamp down on him, begin milking him, and he threw his head back and growled. Then he began moving, pumping into her, thrusting over and over again until her climax hit so hard that he was convinced they would have tumbled to the floor had he not been holding on to her tight.

"Bane!"

"Crystal!"

Never had he wanted any woman more than he wanted her. Nothing had changed. But in a way, things *had* changed. They were older, wiser and in control of who they were and what they wanted. No one could dictate when and where they could love. The sky was now their limit. And as he continued to rock his hips against hers, thrusting in and out of her, working them both into yet another orgasm, he knew that this was just the beginning, just like he'd told her.

He wanted her to feel every hard, solid inch of him; he wanted to rebrand her, reclaim her. And when another climax hit them both, this one more earth-shattering and explosive than the last, he met her gaze just moments before claiming her mouth, kissing her with a hunger he knew she felt. The ecstasy was bone-deep, mind-blowing, erotic.

And when he released the kiss and she screamed his name once again, he knew that no matter what, Crystal Gayle Newsome Westmoreland was his destiny. He knew it with all his heart.

Fourteen

Crystal slowly opened her eyes and squinted against the bright morning sun coming through the open window blinds. She shifted her gaze to Bane, who was down on the floor doing push-ups. She watched and listened to him keeping count. He was up to three hundred and eighty and his entire body was glistening with sweat. She dragged in a deep breath, thinking the man had more energy than anyone she knew.

That was just the beginning...

He had been deadly serious when he'd issued that warning last night. He had proved that yes, he could still make her come with his tongue. Nothing had changed there. And what he was packing between those fine legs of his wasn't so bad, either. She had barely recovered from one orgasm before he'd had her hurling into another. She didn't recall him having the ability to do all that before. At least not in such rapid succession.

She switched her gaze to the clock on the nightstand and saw that it was almost nine. She had slept late and didn't have to wonder why. It had been a late night and early morning with Bane. He had the ability to make her body want him over and over again, to satisfy her each and every time.

This morning she felt sore, but at the same time she felt so gratified and contented she had to force back a purr. She couldn't stop smiling as she shifted in bed to stretch out her limbs, feeling the way her body was still humming with pleasure. If his goal had been to make up for all their lost time, he definitely had succeeded.

"Good morning. It's nice seeing you smile this morning."

She glanced back at Bane. His deep, husky voice sent erotic shivers down her spine. He had finished exercising and was standing across the room with a cup of coffee in his hand. His feet were braced apart, his sweats hung low on his hips and his chest was bare.

"Good morning to you, too, Bane. You gave me a lot to smile about last night," she said honestly.

"Glad you think so."

From his smile she knew he was pleased by her admission. She saw no reason to pretend regret when there wasn't any. And Bane of all people knew there had never been a shy bone in her body. However, seeing him two days ago after all those years had given her pause. She had to take things slow and get to know him all over again. It would be a process and, as far as she was concerned, making love was part of the process.

"I wanted to wait for you to wake up before ordering breakfast," he said, placing the coffee cup aside to come sit on the edge of her bed.

She pulled herself up, being careful to keep the

bedsheet over her naked body. "You didn't have to do that. I'm sure with everything…and especially those exercises…that you must be hungry."

"Starving."

"Then, let's order."

"Okay, but this first."

He leaned down and pulled her into his arms. It didn't bother her one iota that her naked body was revealed in the daylight. She recalled having a problem with Bane seeing her naked before since she'd always thought she didn't have enough curves to show off. Now she did.

He kissed her and she wrapped her arms around his neck and returned the kiss. She could feel every hard inch of him, all solid muscles, and immediately thought back to last night. Her pulse began hammering inside her veins. Only his kisses had the ability to do that to her. If she didn't put a halt to things, she was liable to short-circuit. Like she had last night.

Typically, she wasn't a demonstrative person, not in the least. However, last night had been a different story. She could blame it on the fact that she'd gone a long time without having sex, and once she was getting some, she was like a woman starving for more and more. Bane was a man who had no problem delivering, and she had experienced one orgasm after another. Yes, she could definitely say last night had been off the charts in more ways than one.

She broke off the kiss at the sound of her stomach growling. She chuckled. "I guess that's my tummy's way of letting me know it needs to be fed."

"Then, I'll order breakfast," Bane said, standing and reaching for the phone on the nightstand. "Anything in particular that you want?"

"Pancakes if they have them. Blueberry ones prefer-
ably. Maple syrup and bacon. Crisp bacon. A scrambled
egg would be nice and a glass of orange juice."

He looked at her and grinned. "Anything else?"

"Umm, not at the moment. And while I'm waiting,
I'll take a shower and put on some clothes."

"If you want to walk around naked, I wouldn't mind."

After last night she could definitely see where he
wouldn't mind. "I'd rather put on clothes."

"Your choice."

As he placed their order, she slipped out of bed and
looked around for the clothes he'd taken off her last
night. But she didn't see them. When she found his
T-shirt under a pillow she slid it over her head.

"Nice fit."

She looked down at herself. "It will do in a pinch."
She looked back at him. "Any calls this morning?"

"No. I think we got enough excitement yesterday."

She nodded as she began pulling clean clothes from
her luggage. "What are the plans for today?"

"We stay here most of the day and rest up. When it
gets dark then we'll leave."

"And go where?"

"We'll meet up with my cousins Quade, Dare, Clint
and Cole near the Alabama-Georgia border."

She nodded, recalling having met those particular
cousins at a family get-together around the time that the
Denver Westmorelands had discovered they had rela-
tives living in Georgia, Texas and Montana.

Crystal glanced over her shoulder. Bane was back
to doing his exercises, and the woman in her couldn't
help but admire the way his muscular hips rocked while
he ran in place. Drops of perspiration trickled off his

face and rolled down his neck and shoulders toward his bare chest.

She drew in a deep breath as she imagined her tongue licking each drop and the way his skin would taste. But she wouldn't stop there. She would take her hands and run them all over his body, touching places she might have missed out on last night, although she doubted there were any. She had been pretty thorough.

But still...

What if there were places she had missed and—

"Anything wrong?"

She blinked and realized she'd been standing there staring. Swallowing deeply she said, "No, nothing is wrong." She wanted to turn and rush off toward the bathroom to take her shower, but for some reason she couldn't get her feet to move. It was if they were glued to the floor.

Now he was the one staring at her. She could actually feel his gaze on every part of her. Any place it landed made her body sizzle. She closed her eyes to fight off the desire that threatened to overwhelm her but when she saw it was no use, she opened them again and let them roam over every single, solid inch of him. He was so muscular, and so big and hard. She glanced down at his middle. Umm, did she say big and hard?

She drew in a deep breath when she saw him moving slowly toward her. She wanted to back up but again her feet wouldn't cooperate. All she could do was stand there and watch all six foot three of him gaining ground on her. She felt herself breathing faster with every step he took and her hands actually began shaking. Her fingertips were even tingling, but what she noticed most of all was how the juncture of her thighs seemed to throb like crazy.

When had her desire for him become so potent? Had making love to him all night suddenly turned her into a lustful woman? A woman whose needs dictated how she behaved with him? She could only imagine. But then she thought, no, she really couldn't. She hadn't been with a man taking up her space and time for so long, she wasn't sure how to deal with Bane now.

"Are you sure nothing is wrong, Crystal?" Bane had come to a stop directly in front of her. He was standing so close it wouldn't take much to reach out and touch him, feel those hard muscles, that solid chest glistening with sweat.

"Nothing's wrong, Bane. I'm fine."

He gave her a knowing grin, which put her on notice that he knew she was lying. She wasn't fine. Thanks to him she had gotten a taste of what she'd been missing for five years, and just how well he could still deliver. But it was more than just sex when it came to him. She'd always known it, ever since they'd held out those two years before even making love.

During that time they had developed a closeness and an understanding she knew very few couples shared. She had thought that maybe it hadn't survived their separation, but it seemed to have. Of course she knew better than to expect everything to go back to the way it had always been between them. They weren't the same people. They still needed to work out a few things, make adjustments and get a greater understanding of who they were now. But it could be done.

"May I offer a suggestion?" he asked her.

She licked her lips. It was either doing that or giving in to temptation and leaning over and licking him. "What?"

"Let's shower together."

Now, why had he suggested that? All kinds of hot and searing visions begin flooding her brain. "Shower together?"

"Yes. I suggested that same thing the night before last but you sort of turned me down."

Yes, she had. "I wasn't ready."

He took a step closer. "What about now, Crystal? Are you ready now? After last night, are you ready to give your husband some more playtime?"

It wasn't his request that caused her mind to shatter. It was his reference to himself as *her* husband. Because at that moment it hit her that he was hers and had been since her eighteenth birthday, probably even before then.

Bane had always told her she was his, regardless of what her parents or his family thought about it. And she had believed him. At no time had she doubted his words. Until that day he'd called to tell her he had decided to go into the navy. But now he was back and was letting her know that although he might have changed in some ways, he was the same in the way that mattered to her. He was still hers.

"That shower isn't very big," she decided to say. "And it might get messy with water sloshing all over the place."

"I'll clean it up," he said.

His smile made her weak in the knees, it was so darn sexy. "Well, if you don't mind doing that, then who am I to argue?" And without saying anything else, she forced her feet to move and walked toward the bathroom. But she didn't close the door behind her. When she turned toward the vanity to look in the mirror, out of the corner of her eye she saw that he was still standing in the same spot staring at her. So she figured that she might as well give him something to look at.

"Down boy," Bane muttered under his breath, trying to get his hard-on under control as he watched Crystal strut off toward the bathroom. As he stood there watching, she proceeded to wash her face and brush her teeth. When had seeing a woman doing basic morning tasks become a turn-on? He could answer that easily. The woman was his wife, and the times he'd seen her do those things had been few and far between.

So he watched her and began getting harder. He couldn't help noticing how his T-shirt clung to her breasts as she leaned toward the sink to rinse out her mouth, how the hem of the shirt had inched up and barely covered her thighs. The same thighs he'd ridden hard last night.

And back to her breasts… He could clearly see how hard the buds were and how well defined the twin globes looked. They were a nice size and nice shape. And he knew for certain they had one hell of a nice taste. As far as he was concerned everything about Crystal was nice. The word *nice* wasn't good enough. He could come up with a number of better ways to describe his wife. *Shapely. Sexy. Mesmerizing. Hot. Tasty.*

Did he need to go on? He doubted it. Instead, as he stood there and watched her take a washcloth to wet her face, he was suddenly turned on in a way he'd never been turned on before. Hell, it was worse than last night, and he hadn't believed that could be possible.

Feeling like a man who needed his wife and needed her now, he moved toward the bathroom. She had to know he was coming, but she didn't turn and look his way. Instead, she began removing his T-shirt and then tossed it aside. By the time he reached her she was naked.

Bane moved behind her and looked into the mirror, holding her gaze in the reflection. He moved closer and took hold of her backside, settling his groin against it. Perfect fit. And when he began grinding, feeling his engorged erection working against her buttocks, the contact nearly sent him over the edge. He broke eye contact with her in the mirror to lean over to lap her shoulder, licking it from one end to the other, taking a few nibbles of her flesh in between. He liked the way her skin tasted this morning. Salty. Womanly.

"I haven't taken a shower yet," she whispered in a voice that let him know the effect his mouth had on her.

"We'll eventually get around to it. No rush."

Then he remembered there was a certain spot on her body, right underneath her left ear, that when licked and sucked could make the raw hunger in her come out. So he licked and sucked there and immediately her body began shivering in a way that sent a violent need slamming through him.

"Bane…"

"I know, baby," he whispered. "Trust me, I know. And I want you just as much. Now. I need to be inside you. Bad. I got five years of want and need stored up just for you."

"And last night?" she asked in that same sexy whisper.

"Just the beginning. One night can't alleviate everything. To be honest, I doubt one hundred nights can."

"Oh, my."

"Oh, yes."

And with that said, he turned her around to face him,

lifted her off her feet and sat her on the vanity. "Spread your legs for me, Crystal."

As if they had a will of their own, her thighs parted. He pulled a condom pack out of the side pocket of his sweats and moved back only far enough to ease the sweats down his legs.

"You don't have to use that unless you want to," she said softly. "After I lost the baby my aunt suggested I go on the pill. More to help keep me regulated than anything else."

He nodded. So in other words she was letting him know that this time or any time they felt like it, they could go skin to skin, flesh to flesh. Just the thought made his entire body feel as if it was on fire. "Then, I won't use one."

With his pants out of the way, he got back into position between her spread legs. His shaft was ready, eager to mate and greedier than he'd ever felt it to be. He cupped himself to lead it home.

"Let me."

He looked up and gazed into her eyes. The thought that she'd asked to guide him inside her almost made him weak in the knees. "All right."

When she reached out and took hold of him, he felt himself harden even more in her hands. And then she led him to her center, and it was as if a thousand watts of electricity jolted through her nerve endings to him. And instinctively he pushed forward, thrusting into her hard and deep, all the way to the hilt. Reaching out, he grabbed hold of her hips, and began moving inside her like crazy.

Needing even more of a connection with her, he leaned forward to capture her lips with his. She had the minty taste of whatever mouthwash she'd used and

he intended to lick the taste right from her mouth. She
returned the kiss and he deepened it as much as he
could while thrusting even more deeply into her body.
Setting the same rhythm for both, the same beat. The
same drive.

And the beat went on. He could hear her whispering in a choppy breath for him not to stop. So he didn't.
He couldn't. It seemed that everything was out of his
control. He was out of control. His entire body was
ablaze for her.

"Bane!"

She screamed his name and tightened her legs around
his waist. He thrust harder in response and before he
could catch his next breath, his body exploded. But he
wasn't done.

"Hold on, Crystal. I'm coming again."

"Bane!"

He threw his head back and sucked in a deep gulp
of air that included a whiff of her scent. He practically
lifted her hips off the vanity as he pushed deeper, and
he came again with a primal need that made his entire
body tremble. Now he knew that this woman who'd gotten under his skin so many years ago, who'd been his
world, still was. And would always be so.

Fifteen

There was a knock on their hotel room door. "That should be dinner."

Crystal felt an immediate sense of loss when Bane separated his limbs from hers. Had they gone through breakfast and lunch? A part of her knew they had but the only thing she could recall with clarity was their seemingly nonstop lovemaking sessions. They'd only taken time out to grab something to eat and indulge in a couple of power naps in between.

She watched as he quickly slid into his jeans. When he grabbed his gun off the desk and inserted it into his waistband, it was a stark reminder of the situation they were in. There was a group of people out there who wanted her, and Bane was just as determined that they would not get her.

"Yes?" Bane asked as he looked out the door's peephole.

"Room service."

"Just a minute." He looked over his shoulder at her. "Decent?"

She was pulling his T-shirt over her head. "Now I am." But she still slid beneath the covers and pulled the bedsheet practically up to her chin.

He opened the door to a smiling young woman who couldn't help roaming her gaze all over Bane as she pushed a cart into their hotel room. "Everything you ordered, sir."

"Thanks."

Once the woman left, Crystal slid out of bed and glanced at the food. The cart was set like a table for two. Bane was finally getting his steak and potatoes, and as far as she was concerned, he deserved it. She was certain he'd worked up an appetite over the past few hours.

"I need to wash my hands first."

"So do I."

"But not together. I'll go first," she said, racing off toward the bathroom and closing the door behind her. Every time she and Bane entered the bathroom together they ended up making out all over the place. He had taken her on the vanity and in the shower just before breakfast. And then again in the shower right before lunch.

After washing her hands she quickly dried them off before opening the bathroom door, only to find him standing right there waiting. "My turn now," he said, grinning. "If you want to keep me company, I won't mind."

Yes, she just bet he wouldn't. "No thanks. I'll be okay out here waiting for you. I promise not to start without you."

"I won't be long because I'm sure you're hungry,

too," he said with a grin. He went into the bathroom and closed the door behind him.

Crystal rubbed her hand down her face. Jeez. This new Bane was almost too much for her. He'd always had a pretty hefty sexual appetite, but in the past, due to her lack of experience, he'd always kept that appetite under control. Now it was obvious he wasn't holding anything back. In a way she couldn't help but smile about that because now he was treating her as an equal in the bedroom. He'd taken off the kid gloves and wasn't treating her like a piece of china that could easily break.

"I'm back."

She glanced up and thought that yes, he was back, looking sexy as ever and easily transforming her into one huge bundle of sexual need. "Umm, maybe I should change clothes. Keeping on your T-shirt might not be a good idea."

He moved around her toward the cart. "Don't know why you think so. Besides, we'll both be changing soon enough since we'll be moving out in a few hours."

That was right. He had mentioned that to her. They'd be meeting up with his cousins. When she approached the cart, Bane pulled out a chair for her. She wasn't surprised. One thing about those Westmoreland men, they might have been hell-raisers a time or two, but they always knew how to act proper and show respect.

"Thanks, Bane," she said, taking her seat.

"You're welcome." He leaned down and placed a kiss on her lips. "Eat up."

"Do you know what the plan is after we meet with your cousins?"

He took a sip of coffee and shook his head. "Not sure. Quade has connections with the White House. He may have some insight into the mole at Homeland Security."

Crystal didn't say anything as she began eating, but she couldn't help wondering what could be done to keep her safe. She doubted Bane could continue to protect her on the run. What if he had orders for an assignment? Then where would she be?

"You're frowning. You think the food isn't good or something?"

She glanced over at him. "The food is good," she said of the grilled chicken salad she'd ordered. "I was just wondering about something."

"What?"

"What happens if you get that phone call?"

"What phone call?"

"The one from your commander that you're needed on one of those covert operations."

He shrugged. "Like I told you, my team and I are on military leave for a while. However, if something comes up, I'll let my commander know I can't go. You're my wife and I won't be going anywhere until I know for certain that you're safe."

"Because of your sense of duty and obligation?" she asked, needing to know.

He stared at her as a moment of silence settled between them. Then, he spoke. "I'm not sure what it's going to take for you to realize something, Crystal."

"What?"

"That you're more than an obligation to me. I love you. Always have and always will. That's why I joined the navy five years ago instead of hanging around in Denver and getting into more trouble. In all honesty, I think had I claimed you as my wife back then we might very well be divorced by now."

His words almost snatched the air from her lungs. "Why do you think that?"

"Because there is more to life than what we had back then."

"We had love."

"Yes," he agreed. "And it was our love that would have held things together for a while. But I could see things eventually falling apart. I had a high school education and barely two years of college, and you were determined not to go back to school to get a diploma. All you wanted was to be my wife and the mother of my kids."

"And you saw something wrong with that?" she asked, not sure what he was getting at.

"No, not at the time. But think about it. How far would we have gotten on our own without finally asking your family or mine for help? And eventually I would have resented having to ask anyone for handouts. Granted, I had my land, though legally it didn't belong to me until I turned twenty-five, which meant we would have had to live in the cabin, but only if Dillon agreed to it. But then I doubt the cabin would have been enough. I would have wanted to build a house just as big as my brothers'. One large enough to raise our kids in."

He paused a moment before adding, "And we talked about having a house full of kids without really giving any consideration to how we would take care of them."

She nodded. Although a part of her didn't want to admit it, she knew what he was saying was true. After her miscarriage she had cried for months because she'd lost his baby. After all, they'd talked so often of having a child together one day. But neither had talked about how they would take care of one financially. She'd known the Westmorelands had money, and her young, immature mind had assumed that whatever she and Bane needed his family would eventually take care of. He was right; all she had wanted to do was marry him and have his babies. And she had hated school. Or so she'd thought. The kids had been mean and hateful and resented her ability to ace every test with flying colors. After a while she'd gotten tired of being the class star and having the haters on her back. She'd finally convinced herself that going to school was a waste of her time. Her family had blamed Bane for that decision but it had been hers and hers alone.

She glanced over at him. He had gotten quiet again as he cut into his steak. *Her Bane*. And then a part of her finally got it. He had loved her back then and he loved her now and had told her so several times since he'd walked through her front door. Bane had wanted to give her a better life five years ago because he loved her enough to believe that she and his kids deserved the best of anything. And to give them that, he had made sacrifices. And one of those sacrifices had been her. But she could finally say she understood why he'd made them.

He had wanted to grow up, but he'd also given her a chance to grow up, as well. And she had. She knew how to think for herself, she had two college degrees and was working on her PhD. That had been a lot to accomplish in five years' time and she had done it thanks to him. He had practically forced her to realize her full potential.

"That steak was good."

She glanced over at his plate. It was clean. "You want some of my salad?'

He shook his head and grinned. "No, thanks. I'm good."

Yes, she agreed inwardly. Bane Westmoreland was definitely good. "Bane?"

He pushed his plate aside and glanced over at her. "Yes?"

"I've finally taken my blinders off, and do you know what I see?"

He leaned back in his chair and stared at her. "No. What?"

"A man who loves me. A man who truly loves me even after five years of not seeing me or talking to me. A man who was willing to give me up to give me the best. And for that I want to give you my thanks."

Instead of the smile she'd expected, she watched as a muscle twitched in his jaw. "I really don't want your thanks, Crystal."

No, he wouldn't want her thanks, she thought. He would want her love. Pushing her chair back, she eased from her seat and went to him. Ignoring the look of surprise on his face, she slid down into his lap and turned around to face him. Wrapping her arms around his neck she leaned up and slanted her mouth over his.

He let her kiss him but didn't participate. That was fine with her because she needed him to understand something with this kiss. She'd know the moment he got it, the moment he understood. So she kissed him, putting everything she had into it, and when she heard his breathless moan, she knew he'd almost gotten it. He then returned her kiss with as much passion as she was giving and she felt his hand slide down to her thighs before moving underneath the T-shirt to caress her naked skin.

She knew things could turn sexual between them real quick if she didn't take control. If she didn't let him know what was on her mind...and in her heart. So she pulled back, breaking off the kiss. But that didn't slow up his hands, which were still moving. One was still underneath her T-shirt and the other was sliding up and down her back, stroking the length of her spine.

"I love you, too, Bane," she whispered against his

lips. "I guess you can say I never knew how much until now. And you never stopped loving me like I never stopped loving you. I get that now."

"No, baby. I never stopped loving you," he whispered back against her lips. Then he tightened his arms around her as he stood with her and headed toward the bed.

After placing her there, without saying a word he tucked his fingers into the hem of the T-shirt she was wearing and took it off her.

She watched him step back and ease his jeans down his thighs and legs. Her gaze roamed up and down his naked form. Good thing she wasn't wearing any panties or they would be drenched. She wanted him just that much. And she could tell from the look in his eyes that he wanted her with all the passion he'd stored up for five years. He'd told her as much a number of times, had proved it last night and all day today. She saw it now while looking at his engorged erection and could hear it in his breathing.

He came back toward the bed, and before he could make another move, she reached out and wrapped her fingers around his swollen sex. It fit perfectly in her hand. "Nice," she said, licking her lips.

She heard Bane groan deep in his throat before saying, "Glad you think so."

"I do. Always have thought so."

When she began stroking him with her fingers, even using her fingernail to gently scrape along the sensitive skin, he threw his head back and released a growl that seemed to come from deep within his gut. And when she leaned down and swirled her tongue over him, she felt his fingers dig through her hair to her scalp. That drove her to widen her mouth and draw the full length of him between her lips.

* * *

Pleasure ripped through Bane to all parts of his body.
Crystal was using her mouth to build a roaring fire inside him. A fire that was burning him from the inside
out. And when she used her fingers to stroke the thatch
of curly hair covering his groin, he could feel his erection expanding in her mouth. That pushed her to suck
on him harder and he fought hard not to explode right
then and there. Instead, he reached down and entwined
his fingers in the silky strands of her hair before wrapping a lock around his fist. And then he began moving
his hips, pumping inside her mouth. The more he did
so the more she stroked him before using those same
fingers to gently squeeze his testicles.

Was she trying to kill him? Did she have any idea
what she was doing to him? Did she know how hard it
was to hold back and not come in her mouth? He knew
if he allowed her to continue at this rate, she was liable
to soon find out.

"Crystal," he whispered, barely able to get her name
past his lips as his heart raced and blood pulsed through
his veins. "Stop, baby. You need to stop now."

She was ignoring him, probably because he hadn't
said it with much conviction. And honestly, there was no
way he could with all the pleasurable sensations tearing
through him. Her desire to please him this way meant
more than anything because even with her inexperi-
ence she was doing one hell of a job making him moan.

When he could no longer hold back, he shouted her
name and tried pushing her away, but she held tight to
his thighs until the last sensation had swept through
his body. He should have felt drained but instead he
felt even more needy. Desperate to get inside her body,

he jerked himself out of her mouth and eased her back on the bed.

He felt her body shudder the moment he entered her. She was wet, drenched to the core, which made it easy to thrust deep, all the way to her womb. Then he positioned them so that her legs were wrapped around his waist and back.

He stared down into her face. "I love you. I love your scent. I love your taste. I loved making love to you. I love coming inside you. And I love being buried inside you so deep it's unreal. Heaven. Over-the-top wonderful."

"Oh, Bane."

He was certain she would have said more, but when he began moving, she began moaning. He lifted her hips and began thrusting in and out of her with rapid strokes, taking her over and over again, and intentionally driving her over the edge the way she'd done earlier to him.

He couldn't get enough of her, and when she screamed his name and he felt the heels of her feet dig deep into his back, he knew she was coming. However, he refused to go there yet. But it was the feel of her inner muscles clamping down on him, trying to pull everything out of him that was the last straw, and he couldn't hold back his explosion any longer.

"Crystal!"

He was a goner as he emptied himself completely inside her, filling her in a way that had his entire body shuddering uncontrollably. He could feel her arms wrapped around him and could hear her softly calling his name. Moments later when the earth stopped shaking and his world stopped spinning, he managed to lift his head to stare down at her before crashing his mouth down on hers.

And the words that filled his mind as he kissed her with a hunger he couldn't contain were the same ones he'd said a number of times recently.

This is just the beginning.

Sixteen

"Wake up, sleepyhead."

Crystal slowly opened her eyes and looked out the car's windshield. They were parked at what appeared to be a truck stop decorated with a zillion Christmas lights that were blinking all over the place, although she could see the sun trying to peek out over the mountains.

They had checked out of the hotel around six the night before, which meant that they'd been on the road for twelve hours or so. They'd only stopped twice for bathroom breaks. Otherwise, most of the time she'd been sleeping and he'd been driving. She had offered to share the driving time, but he had told her he could handle things and he had.

He probably figured she needed her rest and she was grateful for that. Before getting dressed, the two of them had taken a third shower. The third in a single day, but all that physical activity had called for it. Besides, she enjoyed taking showers with Bane. He could be so creative when they were naked together under a spray of water. The memories of all they'd done had her body tingling.

Pulling herself up in her seat, she glanced over at him. "We're here already?"

"Yes, but plans changed. Instead of meeting up at the Alabama-Georgia line, we're meeting here."

She glanced around and lifted a curious brow. "And where is here exactly?"

"North Carolina."

North Carolina? No wonder they were surrounded by mountains so huge they reminded her of Denver. "Why the change?"

"They preferred meeting at Delaney's cabin but didn't say why. My guess is because it's secluded, and the way Jamal has things set up, you can spot someone coming for miles around."

"I see." And honestly she did. She had met his cousin Delaney once and recalled hearing how she'd met this prince from the Middle East at a cabin in the North Carolina mountains. To make a long story short, the two had fallen in love and married. "I read an article about her in *Essence* a couple of years back."

"Did you?"

"Yes. And she and her prince are still together."

"Yes, they are. Only thing is that now Jamal is king. He gave the cabin where they met to Delaney as a wedding gift. Since she lives outside the country most of the time, she's given us permission to use it whenever we like."

Bane's phone went off and he quickly pulled it out of the pocket of his jacket and answered it. "This is Bane." After a few seconds he said, "We're here." Then several moments later he said, "Yes, I recall how to get there. I'll see you guys in a little while."

After he hung up the phone he glanced over at her. "I know this has to be both taxing and tiring for you, Crystal, but hopefully the guys and I will come up with some sort of plan."

She nodded. "Still no word on the whereabouts of those other two chemists?"

"No. None. I spoke to Nick while you were sleeping and he's not sure what the hell is going on now. It seems that with the revelation of a mole in the agency, everyone is keeping their lips sealed."

Crystal figured that didn't bode well for her, since Nick had been Bane's source of information from the inside. She bit back an exasperated sigh and leaned back against the headrest.

"Everything is going to be all right," Bane said, reaching over and taking her hand in his. Not waiting for her to respond he asked, "Did you enjoy yourself yesterday and last night?"

That brought a smile to her lips as the pleasant memories washed over her. Hot and spicy memories that made her nipples suddenly become hard and sensitive against her blouse. "Yes, I did. What about you?"

"Yes, I thought it was nice. Best time I've had in a long time."

She was glad he thought so because she definitely felt the same way. The chemistry they'd always shared had been alive and kicking. It didn't even take a touch between them. A look sufficed. At one point he'd lain across his bed and she'd lain across hers with the television going. She had been trying to take a power nap and had felt his gaze on her. When she'd looked over at him and their eyes connected, she couldn't recall who had moved first. All she knew was that the glance had sparked a reaction between them. A reaction that had them tearing off their clothes again.

He brought her hand to his lips and kissed her fingers. "I can't wait to get you back home."

"Home?" She thought of her house that had been set on fire.

"Yes, back in Denver."

She nodded. Although she realized there was nothing back in Dallas for her now, it had been a long time since she'd thought of Denver as home. "What's the hurry?"

"I can't wait for everyone to see you, and to finally introduce you to them as my wife. And we'll have a house to design and build."

Instead of saying anything, she met his gaze and couldn't ignore the flutter that passed through her stomach or the way her pulse quickened at that precise moment. She watched his gaze roam over her, and noticed how his eyes were drawn to her chest. Specifically, the hardened buds pressing against her blouse.

Releasing her hand he turned on the car's ignition. "Come on. We better find Delaney's cabin, and if I figure right, it's about a half hour drive from here. If it was left up to me we'd check into another hotel and have another play day."

Crystal glanced over at him. His eyes were on the road and he was concentrating on their surroundings. She should be, too, but at the moment she couldn't help but concentrate on him.

Brisbane Westmoreland had always seemed bigger than life to her. The past five years hadn't been easy for either of them, but they were back together and that was all that mattered. Now, if they could only stop the men who were trying to kidnap her, everything would be great.

When he brought the car to a stop at a traffic light he glanced over at her and smiled. "You okay, baby?"

She nodded, smiling back at him. Releasing her seat belt, she leaned toward him and placed a quick kiss on his lips. "You're here with me, and as far as I'm concerned that's all that matters now."

She rebuckled her seat belt and sat back. Satisfied.

"What the hell?" Bane muttered through clenched teeth.

Crystal looked over at him and then sat up straight in her seat and glanced out the SUV's window. "What's wrong, Bane?"

He shook his head and stared out at all the cars, trucks and motorcycles that were parked in front of the cabin they'd pulled up to. "I should have known."

"Should have known what?"

"That it would be more than just Quade, Dare, Clint and Cole meeting us today. Some Westmorelands will find just about any excuse to get together."

Chuckling, he brought the car to a stop and turned off the ignition before unbuckling his seat belt. He then reached over and unbuckled hers. "Before going inside, there's something I need to give you."

"What?"

"This," he said, pulling a small black velvet box from his jacket. When he flipped open the lid, he heard her breath catch at the sight of the diamond solitaire ring with a matching gold wedding band.

"Oh, Bane, it's beautiful."

"A beautiful ring for a beautiful woman," he said,

taking the ring out of the box and sliding it on her finger. "It looks good on you, as if it's where it belongs."

She held up her hand and the diamond sparkled in the sunlight. "But when did you get it? How?"

He smiled. "I got it in New York. I had a layover there for a couple of days due to bad weather, and to kill time I checked out some of the jewelry stores. When we got married I couldn't afford to give you anything but this," he said, reaching out and touching the locket she still wore. "I figured it was time I get you something better. It was time I put my ring on your finger."

He got quiet for a moment and then said, "You don't know how much it bothered me knowing you were out there not wearing a ring. I wondered how you were keeping the men away."

"I told you what they thought."

Yes, she had, which he still found hard to believe, but at least it had kept the men at bay.

He lifted her hand and brought it to his lips and kissed it. He then leaned over and lowered his head to kiss her. And he needed this kiss. He hadn't made love to her in over twelve hours, and it was too long.

How had he gone without her for five years? That showed he had willpower he hadn't known he had.

And the one thing he liked most about kissing her was the way she would kiss him back, just like he'd taught her all those years ago to do. Some women's mouths were made for kissing, and he thought hers was one of them. She tasted just as good as she looked and smelled. And that was another thing about her: her scent. His breath would quicken each and every time he took a sniff of her.

His cousin Zane swore that a woman's natural scent was a total turn-on for most men. It had something to do with pheromones. Bane wasn't sure about all that, but the one thing he did know was that Crystal's scent could literally drive him over the edge. And her scent was a dead giveaway that she wanted him regardless of whether she admitted it or not.

There was a loud knock on the truck's window, and he broke off the kiss to glare at the intruder, who said, "Knock it off, Bane."

Rolling his eyes, Bane returned his gaze to Crystal, mainly to focus on her wet lips. "Go away, Thorn."

"Not until I check you over to make sure you're all in one piece. I'm on my way to a benefit bike race in Daytona and in a hurry, so get out of the car."

Bane shook his head as he eased his car seat back. But then in a surprise move he reached across and pulled Crystal over the console and into his arms. He opened the door with her in his arms and got out.

"Bane! Put me down," Crystal said, trying to wriggle free in his arms.

"In a minute," he said, holding her a little longer before sliding her down his body so her feet could touch the ground.

He then turned to Thorn. "Good seeing you, Thorn."

"Good seeing you, too," Thorn said, giving Bane a bear hug. Thorn then reached out to Crystal and pulled her to him, as well. "You too, Crystal. It's been a while."

Bane watched the exchange and knew Thorn's comment had surprised her. Thorn Westmoreland was the celebrity in the family, a well-known, award-winning motorcycle racer who as far as Bane was concerned also built the baddest bikes on earth. He had several movie stars and sports figures as clients.

Crystal and Thorn had only met once at a Westmoreland family reunion, but Bane knew that when it came to his family, Crystal had assumed they saw her as the reason he'd gotten into trouble all those times.

"Thanks, Thorn. It's good seeing you again, as well," Crystal said, as Bane pulled her closer to his side. "How is your family?"

"Fine. Tara's inside along with all the others."

"And just who are *all* the others?" Bane asked.

No sooner than he'd asked that question, the door to the cabin opened and his family members began filing out. The one person Bane hadn't expected to see was Dillon. His older brother stepped out onto the porch along with their cousin Dare. Bane shook his head, not for the first time, at how much Dillon and Dare favored each other.

Bane smiled as his family kept coming out of the cabin. There was Dare and Thorn's brother Stone, and Quade's brother Jared. And besides Dillon, Bane saw his brothers Riley and Canyon, as well as his twin cousins, Aidan and Adrian. He'd just seen the latter four in Denver for Thanksgiving.

"Hey, what's going on?" he asked chuckling. "Last time I looked, Crystal and I were on the run and not dropping by to socialize."

"Doesn't matter," his cousin Dare said, grinning. "We all wanted to see for ourselves that the two of you were okay."

"And we're ready to take anyone on who thinks they can snatch Crystal away from us," Riley said.

"From *us*?" Bane asked, looking at his brother. He knew that of all his siblings and cousins, Riley had been bothered the most by Bane's relationship with Crystal. Riley was afraid that Bane's quest to find her might prove painful if she hadn't waited for him those five years the way Bane had waited for her.

"Yes. *Us.* She's a Westmoreland and we take care of what's ours" was Riley's response.

Bane looked over at Crystal and pulled her closer to his side. "Yes, she is a Westmoreland."

Quade came forward. "Most of the men arrived yesterday. Figured we would get some fishing in while we waited for you to get here. The women showed up this morning and are out back on the porch frying the fish. First we eat breakfast, then we talk about putting a plan together. There're a couple of others we're waiting on."

Bane wondered who the others were but didn't ask. Instead, he said, "Fried fish in the morning? Hey, lead the way."

Crystal had never felt as much a part of the Westmoreland family as she did now. And she knew she had the women to thank for that. They had oohed and aahed over her ring, telling her how much they liked it and how good it looked on her finger. And they had congratulated her on her marriage to Bane and officially welcomed her to the family.

This was her first time meeting Dillon's wife, Pam. In fact, the last time she'd seen Dillon, he was a single man on a quest to find out more about his great-grandfather Raphel. It seemed that pursuit had landed him right on Pam's doorstep, and it had meant nothing to Dillon that Pam was engaged to marry another man at the time.

And then there was Tara, Thorn's wife, whose sister, Trinity, was married to Bane's cousin Adrian. Crystal thought it was pretty neat that two sisters were married to two cousins. And the same thing went for Pam and her sister, Jillian. Jillian was married to Bane's cousin Aidan. Crystal also enjoyed getting to know

Dare's wife, Shelly, Stone's wife, Madison, Jared's wife, Dana, and Canyon's wife, Keisha.

Quade's wife, Cheyenne, was back home in Charlotte with their triplets—a son and two daughters. The girls had dance class today; otherwise, he said his wife would have come with him.

All the women were friendly and the men were, as well. Crystal fought back tears when they welcomed her to the family in a toast. And when Bane's brother Dillon pulled her aside and said that as far as he was concerned, she'd always been part of the family, and that he was glad she and Bane were back together again, she had to excuse herself for a minute to compose herself. Coming from Dillon, that had meant everything.

After going inside for a quick second to get a beer out of the refrigerator, Bane found her sitting on the dock by the lake. Without saying anything, he pulled her up into his arms. "You okay, baby?"

She looked up at him and nodded. "Yes. Everyone is so nice to me."

He smiled and reached out and caressed her cheek. "And why wouldn't they be nice to you? You're a nice person."

"B-but you and I used to cause your family so many headaches. We did some crazy stuff and got into a lot of trouble."

"Yes." He nodded. "We did. But look at us now, Crystal. I finished the naval academy and I'm a SEAL, and you're just a few months shy of getting your PhD. I think Dr. Crystal Westmoreland will sound damn good, don't you?"

Swiping tears away from her eyes, she said, "Yes. I think so, as well."

"All I'm saying is that you and I have changed, Crystal. We aren't the same people we were back then. We're older, better and more mature, although I'll admit we still have a lot of growing to do. But above all, what didn't change was our love for each other. That's the one thing that remained constant."

Crystal knew Bane was right. Their love *had* been the one thing to remain constant. "I love you, Bane," she whispered.

"And I love you back, baby."

Standing on tiptoe, she slanted her mouth over his, doubting that she could or would ever tire of kissing him. And when he wrapped his arms around her and returned her kiss, she knew she could stay in his arms like that forever. Or maybe not, she thought, when she began feeling weak in the knees.

It was the sound of a car door slamming that made them pull their mouths apart. They both turned to look toward the clearing at the people getting out of the cars that had just pulled up. There were three men and a woman. The only person Crystal recognized was the woman. It was Bane's cousin Bailey.

"I'll be damned," Bane said. "That guy… The one in the black leather jacket sure does look like—"

"Riley," she finished for him. "Riley doesn't have a twin, so who is he?" she asked staring.

"That has to be Garth Outlaw. I never met him but I'd heard how he and his five siblings look just like the Westmorelands. And they *are* Westmorelands. I told you we found out that my great-grandfather Raphel had a son he hadn't known about who was adopted by the Outlaws as a baby."

"Well, if anyone doubts Garth Outlaw is related to your family all they have to do is put him and Riley side by side."

"That's true," Bane agreed. "And the man with Bailey is her fiancé, Walker Rafferty. I wonder why they decided to come here instead of flying back to Alaska. When I talked to her the other day that's where they were headed. And I have no idea who the third guy is. The one in the dark suit."

Bane took Crystal's hand in his. "Come on. Quade is beckoning us to join them."

A few moments later when they reached Quade, introductions were made. Just as Bane said, Riley's lookalike was one of their newfound cousins from Alaska, the Outlaws, and the man with Bailey was her fiancé, Walker. However, the third man, the one in the dark suit, was just what Crystal had figured him to be—a government man. She wasn't surprised when Quade said, "Bane and Crystal, this here is Hugh Oakwood. He was recently appointed by the president to head a special agency under the Department of Defense."

Bane raised a brow. "Department of Defense? I don't understand why this would involve the DOD. Their primary concern is with military actions abroad. The Department of Homeland Security's role is to handle things domestically."

Hugh Oakwood nodded as he glanced from Bane to Crystal. "Typically that would be true, but what's going on here isn't typical. We think we're dealing with an international group. And it's highly likely that some of our own people at Homeland Security are involved. That's why the president has authorized my agency to handle things."

The man glanced around and saw he had an audience. Clearing his throat, he asked, "Is there someplace where we can talk privately?"

Quade spoke up and said, "Yes, come this way, Hugh. I got just the place."

Seventeen

Bane had heard that after Jamal had purchased the cabin for Delaney, he'd hired a builder to quadruple the size of it to expand the kitchen, add three additional bedrooms, three more bathrooms, a huge family room and a study. The spacious study was where they were now.

He couldn't imagine anyone getting any studying done in here. Not with the gorgeous view of the mountains and the lake. And if those two things didn't grab you then there was the room itself, with its oak walls and beautiful rustic decor. A floor-to-ceiling bookshelf took up one wall and another wall consisted entirely of a large plate-glass window.

Bane sat beside Crystal on a sofa facing the huge fireplace. Dillon, Quade, Clint, Cole and Dare grabbed chairs around the room. It seemed that Hugh Oakwood preferred standing, which made perfect sense since he had the floor. It was obvious that everyone was interested in what he had to say.

The man turned to Crystal. "I read the report and you, Dr. Westmoreland, have a brilliant mind."

Bane noticed that everyone's gaze had settled on Crystal and she seemed uncomfortable with all the attention she was getting. They were realizing what he'd always known. His wife was a very smart woman.

Crystal blushed. "I wouldn't say that. And officially I'm not a doctor yet."

"I *would* say that. And it's only a matter of months before you get your PhD. After going over all your research, at least what I have access to, there's no doubt that you'll get it," Oakwood said. "And if you don't mind, although I noted you've never used the Westmoreland name, I prefer using it now."

"No, I don't mind," she said. "Bane and I decided years ago to keep our marriage a secret."

Oakwood nodded. "That in itself might be a blessing in disguise. Because no one knows of your marriage, the group that's looking for you has no leads as to where you might be right now."

He paused a moment, then said, "In your research you've basically come up with a formula to make items invisible. Similar testing and research have been done by others, but it seems you might have perfected it to the degree where it's almost ready to use."

"So what does all this mean?" Bane asked.

"It means that in the wrong hands it can be a threat to national security. Right now one particular terrorist group, PFBW, which stands for People for a Better World, sees it as a way to smuggle things in and out of countries undetected."

"Things like what?"

"Drugs, bombs, weapons, you name it. Right, Dr. Westmoreland?"

Crystal nodded. "Yes. Although there's quite a bit of research that still needs to be done before that can happen."

Oakwood nodded. "PFBW have already nabbed the other two chemists, as you all know, and would have grabbed you if your husband hadn't intervened."

"I got that note from someone as a warning," Crystal said.

"Yes, you did. PFBW started recruiting members a few years ago. But we managed to infiltrate the group. That's the only way we know what's going on. When you join, you join for life and the only way to get out is death. We're lucky that our informant hasn't been identified so far."

He paused a minute and then added, "The best we can figure is that although Jasmine Ross started out as part of the group, somewhere along the way she had a change of heart and is the one who slipped you that note. It seems that she tried to disappear as well but wasn't as lucky as you. They found her."

And Bane was sure everyone in the room was aware of the outcome of that. "My wife can't continue to hide out and be on the run forever."

"I agree," Oakwood said. "The problem we're facing is not knowing who we can trust in Homeland Security. The one thing we do know is that PFBW still wants you, Dr. Westmoreland. You're the missing link. The other chemists' work can only go so far. You have researched a key component they lack, and it's your work that's needed to put their scheme in place."

"Sorry, but they won't be getting her," Bane said through clenched teeth as he wrapped his arms around Crystal's shoulders.

"That's why we have a plan," Oakwood said, finally taking a chair.

"What's the plan?" Bane asked, removing his arm from around Crystal to lean forward.

From the looks exchanged between Quade and Oakwood, Bane had a feeling whatever plan Oakwood had come up with, he wasn't going to like it.

Bane was off the sofa in a flash. "No! Hell no! No one is using my wife as bait!"

Crystal reached out and touched Bane's arm. "Calm down, Bane. It doesn't sound too bad."

Bane stared down at her. "They want to set you up someplace and then tell PFBW where you are so they can grab you and—"

"When they do come for me, it sounds as if Oakwood and his men will be ready to arrest them."

Bane rolled his eyes. As a SEAL, he of all people knew things didn't always go as planned. "But what if something goes wrong? What if they fail to protect you? What if—"

"Their mission is successful?" Crystal asked, still trying to calm her husband down. "I have to take the chance their plan will work. Like you said, I can't be on the run for the rest of my life."

Bane pulled her up into his arms. "I know, baby, but I can't take a chance with your life. I can't have you back just to lose you."

Crystal heard the agony in his voice, but she needed to make him understand. "And I can't have you back just to lose you, either, but every time you'll leave to go on covert operations as a SEAL I'll face that possibility."

"It's not the same. I'm trained to go into risky places. You aren't."

He was right; she wasn't. "But I'll be well guarded from a distance. Right, Mr. Oakwood?"

The man nodded. "Right. And we do have an informant on the inside."

A muscle twitched in Bane's jaw. "Not good enough," he said, bracing his legs apart and crossing his arms over his chest. "She won't be alone. I will be with her."

Oakwood shook his head. "That won't work. The people looking for her expect her to be alone."

Bane frowned. "Damn their expectations. I refuse to let my wife go anywhere alone. At some point they'll suspect she had help. They probably already do from the way we've successfully eluded them up to now. I don't like your plan, Oakwood, and the only way I'll even consider it is if I'm the one protecting my wife."

"May I make a suggestion?" Everyone in the room glanced over at Quade.

"What's your suggestion, Quade?" Crystal asked when it was obvious neither Bane nor Oakwood was going to. Tension was so thick in the room you could cut it with a knife.

"Oakwood ran his idea by me earlier and knowing Bane like I do, I figured he wouldn't go along with it, so I came up with a plan B, which I'm hoping everyone will accept. It still requires using Crystal as bait, but at least Bane will get to stay with her."

Oakwood stared at Quade for a moment and then said, "Okay, what's your plan?"

Quade stood. "Before I explain things, I need to get two other people in here who will be instrumental to the success of this plan. The three of us discussed it last night and feel it will work."

He then went to the door, opened it and beckoned for someone. Moments later, Bailey's fiancé, Walker Rafferty, and the Westmorelands' newfound cousin Garth Outlaw entered the room.

Crystal studied Walker and could see how Bailey had fallen for him. He was a looker, but so was Bane. In Crystal's mind, no man looked better. And Garth Outlaw looked so much like Riley it was uncanny. And she found out that like Walker, Garth was an ex-Marine.

Garth began talking. "Quade brought me up-to-date as to what's going on. If you want to set a trap by using Crystal as bait then I suggest you do it in Alaska."

"Alaska?" Bane asked, frowning. "Why Alaska?"

"Because the Outlaws happen to own a cabin on Kodiak Island and it's in a very secluded area. But it's also secured and the cabin has an underground tunnel," Garth said.

Quade moved forward. "If word intentionally leaks out as to where Crystal is, then the people wanting her won't lose any time going after her."

"In Alaska?" Now it was Crystal's turn to ask doubtfully.

"Yes, in Alaska," Oakwood said, rubbing his chin, as if giving plan B serious thought. "They will check things out to make sure it's not a trap, though. Why would Dr. Westmoreland escape to Alaska? The dots will have to connect."

"They will," Garth spoke up and said. "I understand Crystal attended Harvard. Coincidentally, my brother Cash went there at the same time. He was working on his master's degree. Who says their paths didn't cross?"

"I'm following you," Oakwood said thoughtfully. "The people looking for Dr. Westmoreland will assume that their paths *did* cross, and that in desperation, Dr. Westmoreland, you reached out to Outlaw and he offered you safe haven at a cabin he owns in Alaska."

"Exactly," Quade said. "And from what Garth says, this cabin will be perfect. It's in a secluded location on Outlaw property, and the underground tunnel will provide an escape route if needed."

"And in addition to all of that," Garth said, smiling, "thanks to those strong Westmoreland genes, Bane and Cash look alike. Probably just as much as me and Riley resemble each other. That will work in our favor if someone knows Crystal had help and has gotten a glimpse of the guy she's been seen with. They would expect that same guy to be there with her, still protecting her. They will think it's Cash when it will be Bane."

Dillon spoke up. "That plan will work if no one knows that Crystal is married to Bane. Are you guys absolutely certain no one knows?"

"So far that's a guarded secret," Oakwood said. "I checked and Dr. Westmoreland never indicated Brisbane Westmoreland as her husband on any official school records or other documentation. I wasn't even aware of the marriage until Quade brought it to my attention. However, on the other hand," he said, shifting in his chair, "Brisbane Westmoreland has always indicated on any of his official paperwork that he was married and Crystal Newsome Westmoreland is listed as his wife."

Bane shrugged. "I needed to make sure Crystal was taken care of if anything ever happened to me," he said, pulling her closer to him and placing a kiss on her forehead. "I also have medical coverage on her as well, just in case she ever needed it, and I established a bank account in her name."

"All traceable if someone really started to dig," Dare said. It was obvious his former FBI agent's mind was at work.

"Let's hope no one feels the need to dig that far,"

Clint Westmoreland said. He then looked over at Oak-wood. "Can't that information be blocked?"

"Yes, but because I don't know who's the mole at Homeland Security and how high up in the department he or she is, blocking it might raise a red flag," Oak-wood said. "Our main goal is to try to flush out the mole. Right now he is a danger to our national security. To know he might be someone in authority is even more of a reason for concern."

Neither Bane nor Crystal said anything as everyone looked over at them. The decision was theirs.

"It's a big decision. You might want to sleep on it," Cole suggested.

Crystal stood. "Thanks, but there's no need to sleep on it. And I appreciate everyone wanting to help me. However, what concerns me more than anything is that those people want me alive, but they won't think twice about taking out Bane if he gets in their way. For that reason, I prefer that Bane not be with me."

"Like hell!"

When Bane stood up to object further, Crystal reached out and placed a finger over his lips. "I figured that would be your reaction, Bane." She shook her head. "There's no way you'll let me put my life at risk without trying to protect me, is there?"

He removed her finger from his lips and stared down at her with an unwavering expression on his face. "No."

She released a deep breath. "Then, I guess that means we'll be together in Alaska."

A gusty winter's breeze caused Bane to pull his jacket tighter as he wrapped his arms around Crystal and they walked inside the hotel. It was late. Close to midnight. After making the decision that they would be traveling to Alaska, they'd needed to put in place concrete plans. Crystal had trusted him to handle things and asked to be excused to join the ladies who'd been outside sitting on the patio.

In a way he was glad she'd left when she had, because more than once he'd ripped into Oakwood. Too often it appeared that the man was so determined to find out the identity of the mole at Homeland Security that he was willing to overlook Crystal's safety. And Bane wasn't having that.

It had taken Dillon, Quade and Dare to soothe his ruffled feathers and remove the boiling tension in the room by assuring him that Crystal's safety was the most important thing. Only after that could they finally agree on anything.

He still didn't like it, but more than anything he wanted to bring those responsible to justice so that he and Crystal could have normal lives…something they hadn't had since the day they married.

"You've been quiet, Bane," Crystal said a short while later after they'd checked into the hotel and gone to their room.

"Been thinking," he said, glancing around at the furnishings. They were staying at the Saxon Hotel, and it was as if they'd walked right into paradise.

Dare had offered them the use of one of the bedrooms at Delaney's cabin, but since some of his kin also planned to stay there for the night, he had opted out. He preferred having Crystal to himself, and was not up to sharing space with anyone, not even his family. After he said that he and Crystal would spend the night at a hotel in town, Quade had offered him his room at the Saxon Hotel. The penthouse suite.

It just so happened Quade's brother-in-law was Dominic Saxon, the owner of the luxurious five-star Saxon Hotels and the Saxon Cruise Line. Quade had a standing reservation at any Saxon Hotel, but since his wife, Cheyenne, hadn't accompanied him on this trip, he preferred hanging out with his cousins and brother at the cabin, figuring a card game would be taking place later.

"Wow! This place is simply gorgeous," Crystal said.

Bane leaned back against the door as she walked past him to stand in the middle of the hotel room and glance around.

"Yes, it is that," he said, thinking the room wasn't the only gorgeous thing he was looking at. Before leaving the cabin she had showered and changed clothes. Now she was wearing a pair of dark slacks and a pullover sweater. Whether she was wearing jeans and a T-shirt or dressed as she was now, as far as he was concerned, she was the epitome of sexy.

Since her original destination had been the Bahamas, most of the items she'd packed were summer wear. Luckily she and Bailey were similar in size and height, so Bailey had loaned Crystal several outfits that would be perfect for the harsh Alaska weather.

"Come on, let's explore," she said, coming back to him, grabbing his hand and pulling him along.

He wished this could have been the kind of hotel he'd taken her to on their wedding night. As far as he was concerned, it was fit for a king and queen. There was a state-of-the-art kitchen, and according to the woman at the check-in desk, the suite came with its own chef who was on call twenty-four hours a day.

Then there was the spacious living room with a beautiful view of the Smokey Mountains. He figured the furnishings alone in the place cost in the millions. There was a private bar area that came with your own personal bartender if you so desired, and a connecting theater room that had box-office movies at the press of a button.

But what really had his pulse racing was the bedroom, which you entered through a set of double doors. The room was huge and included a sitting area and game nook. He was convinced the bed was created just for lovemaking. Evidently Crystal thought so, as well. He watched as she crossed the room to sit on the edge of the bed and bounced a few times as if to test the mattress.

"It will work."

He lifted a brow, pretending he didn't know what she was referring to. "Work for what?"

"For us. I think that last hotel probably had to replace the mattresses on the beds after we left."

He chuckled, thinking he wouldn't be surprised if they had. He and Crystal had definitely given both beds major workouts. He continued to stare across the room at her. There was just something about seeing Crystal sitting on the bed that was causing a delicious thrill to flow through him. When their gazes met and held, he decided there was something missing from the picture of her sitting on the bed.

Him.

Eighteen

Crystal leaned back on her arms and gazed through watchful eyes as Bane moved from the doorway and headed in the direction of the bed. Straight toward her.

As much as she tried, she couldn't dismiss the flutter in her tummy or the way her pulse was beating out of control. All she could do was watch him, knowing what he had in mind, because it was what she had in mind, as well. He was taking slow, sexy and seductive steps with an intensity that filled the room with his sexual aura. There seemed to be some kind of primitive force surrounding him and she could only sit there, stare and feel her panties get wet.

As if he knew what she was thinking, what she wanted, without breaking his stride he eased his leather jacket from his shoulders and tossed it aside. Next came his shirt, which he ripped from his body, sending buttons flying everywhere. And without losing steam he jerked his belt through the loops and tossed it in the air to land on the other side of the room.

Without a belt his jeans shifted low on his hips, and she couldn't keep her eyes from moving from his face to his chest to trace the trail of hair that tapered from his chest down his abdomen to disappear beneath the waistband of his jeans.

And then there was what he was packing between those muscular thighs of his. She had seen it, touched it and tasted it. And what made her body tingle all over was knowing it was hers.

She studied Bane's face and saw the intensity etched in his features. A few more steps and he would have made it to the bed. And to her. It seemed the room was quiet; nothing was moving but him and he was a man with a purpose.

By the time he reached her she was a ball of desire, and his intoxicating scent—a mixture of aftershave and male—wasn't helping matters. Her head began spinning and she could actually feel her nipples tighten hard against her sweater, and the area between her legs throbbed mercilessly.

"Do you know what I love most about you?" he asked her in a low, husky voice.

"No, what?" She was barely able to get the words out.

"Every single thing. I can't just name one," he said, gazing down at her. "And do you know what I was thinking while standing there watching you sit on this bed?"

"No, what were you thinking?" He was asking a lot of questions and she was providing answers as best she could. Her mind was struggling to keep up and not get distracted by the masculine physique standing directly in front of her. Shirtless, muscular and sexy as sin.

"I was thinking that I should be on this bed with you."

"No problem. That can be arranged. Join me."

She watched his eyes darken. "If I do, you know what's going to happen."

"Yes, but we're making up for lost time, right?"

"Right."

"In that case." She slowly scooted back on the bed. "Join me," she invited again.

In an instant he was bending over to remove his shoes and socks. Straightening, his hands moved to the snap of his jeans and she watched as he pulled his jeans and briefs down his legs.

When he stood stark naked looking at her, he said, "You got too many clothes on, Crystal."

A smile touched her lips. "Do I?"

"Yes."

She chuckled. "And what, Bane Westmoreland, are you going to do about it?"

Hours later Crystal opened her eyes and adjusted to the darkness. The only light she could see was the one streaming in through the bedroom door from the living room. The bed was huge but she and Bane were almost on the edge, chest to chest, limb to limb. She didn't want to wake him but she needed to go to the bathroom.

He wasn't on top of her but he might as well have been. With his thigh and leg thrown over hers, he was definitely holding her hostage. When she tried untwining their limbs to ease away from him, his eyes flew open.

"Sorry, didn't mean to wake you."

He stared down into her eyes and she stared back into his. They were sleepy, drowsy, satisfied. He tightened his hold on her. "And where do you think you're going?"

"The bathroom."

"Oh."

He released his tight hold on her and rolled to the side. "Don't be gone too long. I'll miss you."

She smiled when he closed his eyes again. She quickly searched for her clothes but didn't see them anywhere and didn't want to turn the lamp on to look for them further. So she decided to cross the room in the nude, something he'd done plenty of times.

Moments later after coming out of the bathroom, she decided to go through her luggage to find something to put on. Their bags were just where they'd left them, not far from the door. She was able to see in the light coming from the sitting room, so it didn't take her long to open her luggage and pull out one of her nightgowns. After slipping it on she noticed the satchel Bane had given her.

Not feeling sleepy, she decided now would be a perfect time to read. Opening the satchel, she saw Bane had placed the letters and cards in stacks so she could read them in order. He had also banded them together and labeled them. She grabbed the ones marked My First Year.

She decided to sit on the sofa in front of the fireplace. Using the remote, she turned it on and the bright glow and the heat gave her a warm cozy feeling.

Settling on the sofa with her legs tucked beneath her, she opened the first letter and began reading…

Crystal,

I made it to the navy training facility in Indiana. The other recruits here are friendly enough but I miss my brothers and cousins back home. But more than anything, I miss you. A part of me knows I need to do this and make something of myself for you, as well as for myself, but I'm not sure I can handle our separation. We've never been apart before, and more than once I wanted to walk out and keep walking and return to Denver and confront your parents to find out where they sent you. I want to let them and everyone know you are my wife and that I have every right to know where you are.

But on those days I feel that way, I know why I am enduring the loneliness. It's for you to reach the full potential that I know you can reach. You are smart. Bright. And you're also pretty. I want you to make something of yourself and I promise to make something of myself, as well.

Not sure if you will ever read this letter but I am hoping that one day you will. Just know that you will always have my heart and I love you more than life itself and I'm giving you space to come into your own. And the day I return we will know the sacrifice would have been for the best.

Love you always,
Your Bane

Crystal drew in a deep breath and wiped a tear from her eye. *Her Bane.* Putting the letter back in the envelope, she placed it aside and picked up a Valentine's Day card. She smiled after reading the poem and when she saw how he'd signed the card, "Your Bane" once again, she felt her heart flutter in her chest.

She kept reading all the cards and letters in the stack. In them he told her how his chief had noted how well he could handle a gun, and how he could hit a target with one eye closed or while looking over his shoulder. "Show-off," she said, grinning as she kept reading. His extraordinary skill with a weapon was what had made him stand out so much that his chief had brought it to the attention of the captain who had recommended him for the SEAL program.

She also noted that although her birthday and their wedding anniversary were the same day, he'd bought her separate cards for each. By the time she had finished the first stack she felt she knew how that first year had gone. His first year without her. He had been suffering just as much as she had. He had missed her. Yearned for her. Longed for her. She felt it in the words he'd written to her, and she could just imagine him lying down at night in his bunk and writing her. He'd told her about the guys he'd met and how some of them had become friends for life.

Crystal was halfway through reading the second stack of cards and letters when she heard a sound. She glanced up and saw Bane standing in the doorway.

"You didn't come back. And I missed you."

At that moment all she could think about was that the man standing there was *her Bane*. Putting the stack of cards and letters aside, she eased to her feet and crossed the room to him. They had been through a lot, were still going through a lot, but through it all, they were together.

When she reached him she wrapped her arms around his waist and said the words that filled her heart. "I love you, Bane."

"And I love you." He then swept her off her feet and into his arms. "I'm taking you back to bed."

"To sleep?" she asked.

"No."

She smiled as he carried her back into the bedroom. Once there he eased her gown off her and tossed it aside before placing her back in bed. "I began reading your letters and cards," she said when he joined her there. "Thank you for sharing that period of time with me. And I kept something for you, as well. A picture journal. I'll give it to you when we get to Alaska."

He stroked a hand down her thigh. "You're welcome, and thanks for keeping the journal for me."

And then he leaned down and kissed her and she knew that like all the other times before, this was just the beginning.

Nineteen

"I can't believe this place," Crystal said, after entering the cabin and glancing around.

Bane knew what she meant because he could barely believe it, either. The cabin was huge, but it wasn't just the size. It was also the location and the surroundings, as well as how the cabin has been built with survival in mind.

They had arrived in Kodiak, Alaska, a few hours ago after spending another full day in North Carolina. They had been Garth's guests on his private jet owned by Outlaw Freight Lines. Garth's three brothers—Cash, Sloan and Maverick—had met them at the tiny airport. Their brother Jess, who was running for senator of Alaska, was currently on the campaign trail and their sister, Charm, had accompanied their father to Seattle on a business trip. Garth had joked that it was business for their father and a shopping expedition for their sister.

As far as Bane was concerned, Garth hadn't been lying when he'd said that there was a strong resemblance between him and Cash. The similarity was uncanny in a way. And the similarities between the Westmorelands and the Outlaws didn't end there. In fact, Sloan closely resembled Derringer, and Maverick favored Aidan and Adrian. The Outlaws had easily accepted their biological connection to the Westmorelands, but according to Garth, their father had not. He was still in denial and they didn't understand why.

After making a pit stop at Walker's ranch to drop off Bailey and Walker, Garth and his brothers had driven them on to the Outlaw cabin, which was deep in the mountains and backed up against the Shelikof Strait, a beautiful waterway that stretched from the southwestern coast of Alaska to the east of Kodiak.

"Let us show you around before we leave," Garth said. He and his brothers led them from room to room, and each left Bane and Crystal more in awe than the last. And then the Outlaw brothers showed them the movable wall that led to an underground tunnel. It was better than what Bane had expected. It was basically a man cave with living quarters that included a flat-screen television on one of the walls. The sofa, Bane noted, turned into a bed. The pantry was filled with canned goods. Then there was the gun case that probably had every type of weapon ever manufactured.

"Our grandfather was a gun collector," Sloan Outlaw explained. "Our father didn't share his passion so he gave them to us to get rid of. He has no idea we kept them. As far as we were concerned, they were too priceless to give away."

"Of course, over the years we've added our own favorites," Maverick said, grinning, pointing to a .458 caliber Winchester Magnum, a very powerful rifle. "That one is mine. Use it if you have to."

A short while later, after the tour of the cabin ended, they had returned to the front room. Bane looked over at Cash, the cousin whose identity he would assume for a while. "Hope I'm not putting you out, man."

Cash smiled. "No problem. I need a few days away from Alaska anyway. A couple of friends and I are headed for Bermuda for a few days. Hate how I'll miss all the action."

The plan was to lead the group looking for Crystal to assume that she was in the cabin with Cash, an old college friend. But in order for that plan to work, in case someone went digging, the real Cash Outlaw needed to go missing for a while.

Oakwood would be calling in the morning to give Bane the final plans and let him know when word of Crystal's whereabouts would be leaked so they could be on guard and get prepared. The DOD already had men in place around the cabin. They had been there when Bane and the group arrived. Other than Garth, no one had noticed their presence, since they blended in so well with the terrain.

A short while later Bane and Crystal were saying goodbye to everyone. After Bane closed the door behind him, he looked across the room at Crystal. He thought she was holding up pretty damn well for a woman who in the next twenty-four hours would be the bait in an elaborate trap to catch her would-be kidnappers. As soon as the DOD purposely leaked her whereabouts, it would set things in motion.

"I like them."

He saw her smile. "Who?"

"Your cousins."

"And what do you like about them?" he asked, moving away from the door toward her.

"For starters, how quick they pitched in to help. They didn't have to offer us the use of this place."

"No, they didn't. Garth and his brothers paid a visit to Colorado the week before Thanksgiving to meet the Denver Westmorelands and from there they headed south to visit with the Atlanta Westmorelands. Dillon told me I would like them when I met them and I do."

He drew her into his arms. "If we pull this off we'll owe them a world of thanks. This place is perfect, and not just because of the underground tunnel. There's also the location, the seclusion. I can see someone hiding out here, and I'm sure the people looking for you will see it, too."

"I wonder when Oakwood will send his men," she said thoughtfully, looking up at him.

Bane chuckled. "They're already here."

Surprise appeared on her face. "What? Are you sure?"

"Pretty much. I haven't seen them but I can feel their presence. I noticed it the minute we pulled up in the yard. And because Garth is an ex-Marine, he did, too."

"He said something to you about it?"

Bane shook his head. "He didn't have to. He knew what to look for." Bane didn't say anything for a minute and then he said, "Nothing can happen to you, Crystal. I won't allow it. Do you know what you mean to me?"

She nodded and reached up to place her arms around his neck. "Yes, I know." And she really did. Reading those cards and letters had left her in awe at the magnitude of his love for her.

"Good." And then he leaned down and captured her mouth with his.

* * *

Later that night, just as before, Crystal untangled herself from Bane and slid out of bed. At least she tried. But Bane's arms tightened around her. "Where are you going?"

"To read. I'm on stack three now."

He rolled over in bed so they could lie side by side. "Interesting reading?"

"I think so," she said. "It means a lot knowing you were thinking about me." Reading those cards and letters, especially the letters, had helped her to understand that he loved being a navy SEAL and that his teammates were his family, as well.

"I always thought about you," he said huskily. He rubbed her cheek. "Sleepy?" he asked her.

"No. I plan to read, remember? So let me go."

"Okay, just as long as you're where I can see you."

"I'll just be in the living room."

He shook his head. "Not good enough. I want you in here with me."

She was about to argue with him, remind him the cabin was surrounded by the good guys, but instead she said, "Okay, I'll read in bed if you're sure I won't disturb you."

"I'm sure. I'm wide-awake, as well."

He released her. After slipping back into the gown that he'd taken off her earlier, Crystal padded across the room to pull the third stack out of the satchel.

While getting the cards and letters, she pulled out the photo album she had packed. Going back to the bed, she handed it to him. "Here. This is my gift to you."

Bane took it. "Thanks, baby." He then got into a sitting position and began flipping through the photo album. He came across their marriage license and smiled. When she saw his smile, she said, "We were so young then."

"Yes," he agreed. "But so much in love."

"We still are," she said, settling into position beside him. In amiable silence, he turned the pages of the photo album while she read his cards and letters. "This is your high school graduation picture?" he asked.

She glanced up from reading the letter to look over at the photograph he was asking about. "Yes. And all I could think about that day was that because of you, I had done it. I had gotten the very thing I thought I hadn't wanted and was actually pretty happy about it."

He looked at several more pictures, and when he came to her college graduation picture he said, "Isn't it weird that Cash was there on campus at the same time you were?"

"Yes. I can't imagine what my reaction would have been had I ran into a guy on campus who reminded me of you. So personally, I'm glad our paths didn't cross."

She was about to go back to reading her cards and letters when Bane's cell phone went off. He reached for it. "This is Bane."

Crystal tried reading his expression while he talked with the caller but she couldn't. The only clue she had that he was angry was the way his chin had tightened. And then when he asked the caller in an angry tone, "How the hell did that happen?" she knew something had made him furious. A few moments later he ended the call and immediately sent several text messages.

"What's wrong, Bane?"

He looked over at her and paused before saying anything, and she figured he was trying hard to get his anger in check. "That was Oakwood. Someone in his department screwed up."

He threw his head back as if to get his wrath under control and said, "Your location has already been leaked. The only good thing is that whoever they suspected as the mole took the bait, and he and his men are headed here believing that you're hiding with Cash."

"And the bad thing?" she asked, knowing there was one.

Bane drew in a deep fuming breath. "Whoever this guy is, he's evidently pretty high up there at Homeland Security. He contacted the person in charge of Oakwood's men and gave an order to pull out because a special task force was coming in to take over."

Crystal frowned. "Are you saying Oakwood's men are no longer outside protecting us?"

"That's exactly what I'm saying. But I don't want you to worry about anything. I got this," Bane said, getting out of bed and slipping on his jeans. "What I need for you to do is to go and get in the tunnel below."

"Is that where you'll be?"

"No," he said, picking up his Glock and checking his aim. "I might need to hold things down for a while. Oakwood ordered the men to return and hopefully they'll be back soon."

Crystal didn't want to think about what could happen if they didn't. Bane expected her to be hiding out below, where she would be safe, while he single-handedly fought off the bad guys until help arrived. "I prefer staying up here with you. I may not be as good a shot as you, but thanks to you I'm not bad."

He frowned. "There's no way I can let you stay here with me."

"I don't see why not," she said, sliding out of bed to begin dressing, as well. "To be honest with you, I feel pretty safe."

He shook his head. "And why are you feeling so safe?"

She looked over at him and a smile spread across her lips. "Because I'm not here with just anyone protecting my back. I'm here with Badass Bane."

Twenty

A short while later, Crystal studied the arsenal of Bane's personal weapons spread out on the table and glanced over at him. "I thought a person couldn't travel on a plane with one weapon, much less a whole suitcase full of them."

He met her gaze. "They can't."

She lifted a curious brow. "Then, how did you get through the security checkpoint when you flew to Dallas?"

"I didn't. Bailey figured I might need them and brought them with her to the cabin. I'm glad she did. And there was no problem bringing them with me on Garth's private plane."

Crystal watched how he checked each one out, making sure there was enough ammunition for each. It was close to one in the morning. "You have some awesome teammates, Bane. I enjoyed reading about them, and they have been here for you. For us. Throughout this ordeal. I can't wait to meet Coop. You mentioned him a lot in your letters."

She noticed Bane's hands go still, and when she glanced into his face she saw pain etched in his features. "Bane? What is it? What's wrong?"

He looked at her. "You won't get a chance to meet Coop, Crystal. We lost him during one of our covert operations."

"Oh, no!" She fought back tears for a man she'd never met. But in a way she had met him through Bane's letters and knew from what he'd written that he and Coop shared a special bond. "What happened?"

"I can't give you the details but it was a setup. I'm not sure how it was done but he was taken alive. Then a few days later they sent our CO Coop's bloody clothes and military tag to let us know what they did to him."

She wrapped her arms around Bane's waist. "I am so sorry for your loss. After reading your letters I know what a special friendship the two of you shared."

Bane nodded. "Yes, he was a good friend. Like a brother. I'm sorry you didn't get to meet him."

Hearing the sadness in his words, Crystal leaned up on tiptoe and pressed her lips to his. It was a quick kiss, because they didn't have much time and the situation wouldn't allow anything else. She released him, took a step back and glanced at the clock on the wall. "That's strange."

"What is?"

"I'm surprised no one has called. I would think Oakwood would be keeping tabs on us, letting us know what's going on or how close those people are to here." When Bane didn't say anything she studied his features. "You noticed it, too. Didn't you?"

"Yes, I noticed it and I think I know the reason."

"Why?"

"Someone blocked any calls coming in or out of here. Whoever did it assumes they have us cornered, but I was able to text Walker and the Outlaws right after talking with Oakwood to apprise them of what's going on. I have every reason to believe they are on their way if they aren't here already." He looked down at her. "I'm asking you again to go down below, Crystal."

"Only if we're down there together."

She heard his deep breath of frustration before Bane said, "Then take this," and passed her one of the smaller handguns off the table. "Not that you should need to use it," he added. She inserted it into the pocket of her jacket.

At that moment the light in the room flickered a few times before going completely out, throwing the entire house into darkness. "Bane?"

"I'm here," he said, wrapping an arm around her.

She jumped when suddenly there was a hard knock at the door.

"Seriously? Do they think we plan on answering it?" Bane said in an annoyed tone.

"But what if it's Walker or the Outlaws? Or even Oakwood?"

"It's not," he said. "Too soon to be Oakwood. And as far as Walker and the Outlaws, we agreed to communicate by a signal."

"What kind of signal?"

"The sound of a mourning dove's coo. I didn't hear the signal so you know what that means."

She nodded. Yes, she knew what that meant.

Bane wished like hell that Crystal had done what he'd said and gone down below. He needed to concentrate and wasn't sure he could do that for worrying about her.

Suddenly a loud voice that sounded as if it came through a megaphone blared from outside. "Mr. Outlaw. Miss Newsome. We are members of the Department of Homeland Security. We're here to take Miss Newsome to safety."

"Like hell," Bane whispered in a growl. "Those bastards expect us to just open the door and invite them inside in total darkness. They figure we're stupid enough to fall for that?"

"If you don't respond to our request," the voice continued, "we will assume the two of you are in danger and will force our way in."

Your decision, Bane thought. *Bring it on.*

"You think they really will force their way in?" Crystal asked softly.

"That's evidently their plan, so let's get prepared," he said, lowering her to the floor with him. At that moment his cell phone vibrated in his pocket. Someone had gotten past the block. He quickly pulled the phone out and read the text message from Walker. 5 of them.

"Somehow Walker got through the block to let me know there are five men surrounding the cabin. At least that's all they see. There might be others."

"At least Walker and the Outlaws are here."

"Yes, and they know to stay low and not let their presence be known unless something serious goes down. We need to get the ringleader."

"So for now it's five against two."

He frowned. "I want you to stay down, Crystal. They won't do anything that will harm you since you're valuable to them. That means they'll try to get inside to grab you."

Suddenly there was a huge crash. It sounded like the front door caving in. "Shh," Bane whispered. "Someone just got inside."

* * *

Male voices could be heard from another room. "Miss Newsome, let us know where you are. We know you think you're safe here with Cash Outlaw, but we have reason to believe he can't be trusted. We need to get you out of here and get you to safety."

Multiple footsteps could be heard going from room to room, which meant more than one man had gotten inside. Suddenly the lights came back on. "Stay down," Bane ordered her as he moved to get up from the floor.

"Not on your life." The moment she eased up with Bane, who had his gun drawn, two men entered the room with their guns drawn, as well. Bane shoved her behind him.

"Miss Newsome? Are you okay?" one of the men asked. Both were dressed in camouflage. One appeared to be well over six feet and the other was five-nine or so.

"I'm fine," she said, poking her head from around Bane to size up the two men. Both looked to be in their forties, with guns aimed right at Bane. He in turn had his gun aimed right at them.

"Then, tell your friend to put his gun down," the shorter of the two men said.

"Why can't the two of you put yours down?" Crystal retorted. She tried to block from her mind the sudden thought that this was how things had played out in the dream she'd had a few nights ago.

"We can't. Like we told you, Homeland Security has reason to believe he's dangerous."

As far as Crystal was concerned, that wasn't an understatement. She could feel the anger radiating off Bane. "Who are you?" she asked the one doing all the talking.

"We're with Homeland Security," the taller man said.

"I want names."

She could tell from his expression that he was getting annoyed with her. "I'm Gene Sharrod, head of the CLT division, and this is Ron Blackmon, head of DMP."

"You're both heads of your divisions. I'm impressed. Why would the top brass personally come for me?"

"The people after you want you for insalubrious reasons. Reasons that could be a threat to our national security."

"I got the note."

"Yes, and we believe you did the right thing by disappearing like it told you to. But now we're here to handle things and keep you safe."

Crystal lifted her chin. "How did you know what the note said?" She could tell from the look on the man's face that he realized he'd just made a slip.

"Let's cut the BS." Bane spoke up in an angry voice. "Bottom line is she isn't going anywhere."

"You aren't in any position to say anything about it, Mr. Outlaw," the shorter of the two men said with a sneer. "In case you haven't noticed, there are two guns aimed at you so I suggest you drop yours."

"And I suggest the two of you drop yours," Bane responded tersely, looking from one man to the other.

The taller man had the audacity to snicker. "Do you honestly think you can take the both of us down, Outlaw?"

A cocky smile touched Bane's lips. "I know I can. And the name isn't Outlaw. Cash Outlaw is my cousin. I'm Brisbane Westmoreland. Navy SEAL. SE348907. And just so you know, I'm a master sniper. So be forewarned. I can blow both your heads off without splattering any blood on that sofa."

The shorter man seemed taken aback by what Bane

had said, but Crystal could tell by the look that appeared in the taller man's eyes that he thought Bane was bluffing.

"Trust me," she said. "He's telling the truth."

The taller man's eyes darkened in anger. "We're not leaving here without you."

"Wanna bet?" Bane snarled. "My wife isn't going anywhere with either of you."

"Wife?" Sharrod asked, shocked.

"Yes, his wife," Crystal confirmed, holding up the finger of her left hand, where her diamond ring shone brilliantly.

"I'm tired of talking," Bane said. "Put your damn guns down now."

Blackmon narrowed his gaze at Bane. "Like Sharrod said. You're in no position to give orders."

Suddenly shots rang out and before Crystal could blink, Bane had shot the guns right out of both men's hands. "I am now," Bane said easily.

The two men bowed over, howling in pain. One of them, Crystal wasn't sure which one, claimed one of his fingers had gotten shot off. Then they heard the mourning dove coo just seconds before Walker, Bailey and Garth stormed into the room with their own guns drawn.

"You guys okay?" Bailey asked, rushing over to them, while Walker and Garth went over to the two men, who were wailing at the top of their lungs, sounding worse than babies. "Sloan and Maverick are outside taking care of the men who came with these two."

"You're going to regret this, Outlaw…Westmoreland, or whatever your name is," Blackmon snarled. "Homeland Security is going to nail your ass. This is treason. You are betraying your country."

"No, I think the two of you are betraying yours," Oakwood said, charging in. "Gene Sharrod and Ron Blackmon, you are both under arrest. Get them out of here," he told his men as they rushed forward.

"We need medical treatment," Blackmon screamed, holding his bloodied hand when agents came to grab him.

Bane frowned. "Better be glad it was just your hands and not your damn heads like I threatened to blow off. So stop whining."

After Oakwood and his agents had taken both men out the door, Bane turned to Crystal and frowned. "I told you to stay down."

She reached up to caress the angry lines around his jaw. "I know, but you forgot what you also said."

"What?"

"That we were in this together."

And then she leaned up to place a chaste kiss on his lips, but he evidently had other ideas and pulled her into his arms and deepened the kiss. She wrapped her arms around him and returned the kiss, not caring that they had an audience.

When one of the men cleared his throat, they broke off the kiss and Bane whispered against her moist lips, "Come on, Mrs. Westmoreland. Let's go home."

Twenty-One

A week later

Crystal hadn't meant to awaken Bane. But when he shifted in bed and slowly opened sleepy eyes that were filled with a heavy dose of desire, she saw he was now wide-awake.

She knew of no other man who could wake up ready to make love after going to bed the night before the same way. But then, hadn't he warned her that as far as the intensity of their lovemaking was concerned, this was just the beginning?

"Good morning," he said in that deep, husky voice that she loved hearing.

She smiled. "And good morning to you, too, Bane."

And as far as she was concerned, it was a good morning, especially after that phone call they had received yesterday. According to Oakwood, Sharrod had caved in under pressure and told them everything, including the location where those other two chemists were being held. By now the two men had been reunited with their families.

She glanced around the cabin. Their cabin. Bane had built it years ago for her as their secret lovers' hide-away. Now it was her home. Originally it had just one large room with a bathroom, but last year Bane had instructed Riley to hire someone to add a kitchen nook and a sitting area and to enlarge the bathroom. His sister Gemma, who was an interior decorator, had put her signature on it both before and after the renovations. There was an iron bed in the bedroom with colorful curtains that matched the bedspread.

The sitting room was the perfect size, just large enough for a sofa, a chair and a table. And she loved the fireplace that provided such great heat on those really cold days and nights. There was also a flat-screen television on the wall. Bane told her that he had begun spending his days and nights here whenever he came home. For that reason, he had installed internet services and didn't have to worry about missing calls due to his phone being out of range. Now he could send and receive phone calls just fine.

Already plans had been made to build the house that would become their permanent home. It wouldn't be far from here on Bane's Ponderosa, the name of the spread he had inherited. They would start looking at house plans next week. The one thing they did know was that whatever house they built would have to be large enough for all the kids they planned to have one day.

She had gotten around to reading all his cards and letters, and if she could have loved him even more than she already did, she would have. He had poured out his heart, his soul and his agony of a life without her in it. She needed no further proof that she was loved deeply by the man who was meant to be hers always, just as she was meant to be his.

Yesterday she and Bane had visited her parents' property. Property that was now hers. The place was deserted and badly in need of repairs. However, they'd decided not to make any decisions about what they would do with it for now.

In a way the five years of separation had done what it was meant to do. It had helped them grow into better people. She definitely saw a change in Bane. He could still be a badass when he needed to be, but there was a calmness about him, a discipline, self-control and purpose that hadn't always been there before. He'd always loved her and his family. And now he loved his country with just as much passion.

And his family was wonderful. She was enjoying getting to know the ladies his brothers and cousins had married. She had always been a loner, and for the first time in her life she was feeling part of the family.

Because Crystal had lost a lot of her things in the fire, Pam had organized a welcome-home party for her and Bane where she had received a lot of gift cards. It just so happened they were all from the ladies' favorite places to shop.

And then there was the Westmoreland family tradition. Every other Friday night, the Westmorelands got together at Dillon's place. The women would do the cooking and the men would arrive hungry. Afterward, the men took part in a poker game and the women did whatever they pleased. Usually they planned a shopping expedition. Tonight would be Crystal's first

Westmoreland Family Chow Down, and she was looking forward to it.

Bane shifted his position in bed and Crystal was in-
stantly aware of the erection poking against her backside. Instinctively, she scooted back to bring her body
closer to his. All that desire bottled up inside him was
beginning to affect her, as well. "What happens when
you get tired of me?"

"I won't. You're in my blood, baby. And in my soul.
And especially here," he said, taking her hand and placing it on his chest, right against his heart.

His words touched her deeply. And it didn't help matters that he was staring down at her, seducing her with
those gorgeous hazel eyes. "Oh, Bane." At that moment
she wanted him. "Make love to me."

"It will be my pleasure."

Later that evening Crystal sat beside Bane at the
dinner table at Dillon's home, surrounded by Bane's
brothers, cousins and their spouses. And then there were
the children. A lot of children. Beautiful children who
were the joy of their parents' lives. Seeing them, spending time with them, made her anxious to have a child
of her own. A baby. Bane's baby.

Dillon had made a toast earlier to her and Bane, officially welcoming her to the family and telling them
how proud he and the family were of them, and their
strong and unwavering commitment to each other. He
also gave them his blessings, just as he'd known his
parents would have done, for a long and happy marriage. His words had almost brought tears to her eyes
because she felt she was truly a part of this family. The
Westmoreland family.

A short while later, when dinner was over and the

women were clearing off the table as the men geared up for a card game, Bane's cell phone rang. "It's my CO," he said, quickly pulling his phone out of his jeans pocket. "Excuse me while I take this."

She felt a hard lump in her throat. She knew Bane was on military leave until March. Had something come up where his CO was calling the team together for an assignment? It was three weeks before Christmas. Besides that, it was their first week together without all the drama. Crystal wasn't sure how she would handle it if he had to suddenly leave.

You will handle it the same way any SEAL wife would, an inner voice said. *You will love him, support him and be there with open arms when he returns.* She was suddenly filled with an inner peace, prepared for whatever came next.

"What is it, Bane?" Dillon asked.

Crystal, like everyone else, turned to gaze at Bane when he returned to the dining room. There was a shocked look on his face. Although it had been Dillon who asked the question, Bane met Crystal's gaze and held it.

"That was my CO. He wanted to let me know he got a call from the Pentagon tonight that Coop is alive and is being held prisoner somewhere in Syria."

"Your friend Coop?" Crystal asked, getting up out of her seat and crossing the room to Bane.

"Yes. And the CO is getting our team together to go in and get Coop, and any other hostages they're holding, out of there."

She nodded. "When will you be leaving?" she asked softly.

He placed a hand on her shoulder. "I'm not. The CO just wanted me to know. He's aware of our situation and what we went through last week. He's letting me know he's exempting me from this mission if that's what I want."

Crystal studied Bane's features. And not caring if they had an audience listening to their every word, she said, "But that's not what you really want, is it?"

He rubbed his hand down his face. "Doesn't matter. It's three weeks before Christmas. There's no telling when I might return. I might not make it back until after the holidays, and I wanted to spend every single day with you."

"And I with you. But you *must* go," she said, not believing she was actually encouraging him to do so. "Coop is your best friend."

"And you are my wife."

A smile touched her lips. "I'm also the wife of a SEAL. So things like this are to be expected. I know it and I accept it. I will be fine until you get home, and if you don't make it back by Christmas, I won't be alone. For the first time, Bane, thanks to you I have a family," she said, glancing around the room. "I have a big family."

"Yes, you do," Dillon said, joining the conversation. "And whenever Bane has to go out on covert operations we will be here for you."

"Thanks, Dillon." Crystal returned her gaze to Bane. "So go, Bane, and be the dedicated and fierce SEAL that you are. The one you were trained to be. Be careful and do everything in your power to bring Coop home."

Bane stared at her for a long moment before he reached out and pulled her to him and held her close. And then he leaned down and kissed her with all the love she actually felt. The love she knew was there and had always been there between them. Suddenly she was swept off her feet and into big, strong arms.

"Bane!"

Holding her tight, he headed for the door. "We're going home," Bane said over his shoulder as his whole family watched them. "Crystal and I bid you all a good night."

Twenty-Two

Christmas Eve

"And you're sure you don't want to spend the night at our place, Crystal? You're more than welcome."

Crystal smiled at her brother-in-law when he brought the car to a stop in front of the cabin. "Thanks, Dillon, but I'll be okay."

"I promised Bane I would look out for you."

"And you have. I really do appreciate the invitation, but I'm fine."

She knew she would be a lot better if Bane called, but neither she nor his brothers and cousins had heard from him since he'd left three weeks ago. He had told them that no one knew how long this operation would take. She just hoped he was safe and all was going well.

In the meantime she had tried staying busy. Bane had wanted her to look at house plans while he was gone, and she had helped Pam at her acting school in town. Jason's wife, Bella, had invited her for tea several times, and there had been a number of shopping trips with the Westmoreland ladies. There had been the annual Westmoreland charity ball. It was her first time attending one and she wished Bane could have been there with her. But it had been good seeing the Outlaws again.

And she had been summoned to the nation's capital last week. Dillon, Canyon and their wives had gone with her. She'd had to give a statement about Sharrod and Blackmon. No one had asked about Bane's whereabouts and she figured they knew it was classified information.

The director of Homeland Security had told her of the value of her research and that someone would be contacting her soon. They wanted her, along with the other two biochemists, to come work for the government to perfect their research while she completed her PhD. She promised she would give it some thought but refused to make any decisions until Bane returned.

"I used to worry about Bane whenever I figured he was out on one of those operations," Dillon said softly to her as he unbuckled his seat belt. "But then I figured it didn't pay to worry. Besides, we're talking about Bane, the one person who can take care of himself. If we should be worried about anyone, it's those who have to come up against him."

Crystal smiled, knowing that was true. She had seen how Bane had handled Sharrod and Blackmon. He had been confident, cool and effective, even when it had seemed the odds had been stacked against him.

"Bane will be okay, Crystal," Dillon said when she didn't respond to what he'd said.

She nodded and absently touched the locket she still wore around her neck. "I hope so, Dillon."

"Don't just hope. Believe."

Her smile spread. "Okay, I believe."

"Good."

He got out of the car and came around to open the door for her. "You will be joining us for Christmas breakfast in the morning and then later a special Westmoreland Holiday Chow Down tomorrow night, right?"

"Yes, I'm looking forward to it."

"The Outlaws will be arriving about noon along with Bailey and Walker and some of the Atlanta Westmorelands."

She had gotten the chance to meet Charm Outlaw before she and Bane had left Alaska. Charm and her father had been returning from their business trip. The woman was as beautiful as she was nice. However, Crystal thought the father of the Outlaws had been reserved, as if he'd rather them not be there. Bane had explained that the old man was having a hard time accepting the fact that his father had been adopted.

"You know the drill," Dillon said, grinning when they reached the door of the cabin.

"Yes, I know it." Because she was living in a secluded area, the men in the family refused to let her drive home alone. They either drove her back home or followed behind her in their car to make sure she got there safely. And then before they would leave, she'd have to give a signal that everything was okay by flashing the window blinds.

"Good night, Dillon."

"Good night. Do you need a ride to my place in the morning?"

"No, thanks. I'll drive."

She opened the door to go inside the house and was glad she'd left the fireplace burning. The cabin felt warm and cozy. She was about to turn and head for the window to flash the blinds when she saw a movement out the corner of her eye. She jerked around.

"Bane!"

She raced across the room and was gobbled up in big, strong arms and kissed by firm and demanding lips. It seemed as though the kiss lasted forever as their tongues tangled and mingled, and they devoured each other's mouths. Finally, he broke off the kiss. "I missed you, baby."

"And I missed you," she said, running her arms all over him to make sure he was all in one piece. His skin was damp, he smelled of aftershave and he was wearing his jeans low on his hips. It was obvious he'd just gotten out of the shower.

"Why didn't you let me know you were coming home tonight?"

A smile touched his lips. "I wanted to surprise you. The mission was a success, although it was damn risky at times. They were keeping Coop and two other American prisoners secluded up in the mountains. Getting up there was one thing and getting them out alive was another. It wasn't easy but we did it, and all returned home safely. No injuries or casualties."

He paused a moment and said, "Coop was glad to see us and they didn't break his spirit, although they tried. He said what kept him going was believing that one day we would come rescue him. And we did. He and the others were taken to Bethesda Hospital in Maryland to get checked out."

Crystal was about to open her mouth to say something when there was a loud pounding at the front door. "Oops. That's Dillon. He brought me home and I forgot to flash the blinds to let him know I was okay," she said, racing across the room to open the door.

"Crystal, are you okay? When you didn't flash the blinds I—" Dillon stopped talking when he glanced over her shoulder and saw his brother. "Bane!"

The two men exchanged bear hugs. "Glad to see you back in one piece," Dillon said, grinning as he looked his baby brother up and down.

Bane pulled Crystal to his side and planted a kiss on her forehead. "And I'm glad to be back, too."

"I'll let the family know you're home. And I guess we won't be seeing you bright and early tomorrow morning for breakfast as planned, Crystal," Dillon said, his grin getting wider.

"No, you won't," Bane answered for her. "My wife and I are sleeping in late. We will try to make it for dinner, however."

Dillon chuckled. "Okay." He then looked at his watch. "It just turned midnight on the East Coast. Merry Christmas, you two."

"And Merry Christmas to you, Dillon," Crystal said, cuddling closer in her husband's strong arms. And in that moment she knew that for her this would be the merriest because she had her Bane. It would be their first Christmas spent together as man and wife.

As soon as the door closed behind Dillon, Bane tightened his embrace and looked down at her. "I like the tree and all the decorations."

She glanced over at the Christmas tree she'd put up a couple of weeks ago. What was special about it was that it had come right off Bane's Ponderosa. Riley had chopped it down for her. She'd had fun decorating the tree and had even trailed Christmas lights and ornaments along the fireplace mantel. "Thanks."

And then Bane pulled her even closer into his arms. "I've already placed your gift under the tree, baby."

She glanced over her shoulder and saw the huge red box with a silver bow. She looked back at him, feeling like a kid on Christmas morning. "Thanks. What's in it?"

He chuckled. "You get to open it in the morning." He leaned down and placed a kiss on her lips. "Merry Christmas, sweetheart."

She reached up and wrapped her arms around his neck. "And merry Christmas to you, Bane."

And then their mouths connected, and she knew this was still just the beginning. They had the rest of their lives.

Epilogue

Valentine's Day

"I would like to propose a toast to the newlyweds," Ramsey Westmoreland said, getting everyone's attention and holding up his champagne glass. "First of all, we didn't ever think you would leave us, Bay, but we know you'll be in good hands living in Alaska with Walker. We're still going to miss you showing up unannounced, letting yourself into our homes and eating our food."

"And getting all into our business," Derringer hollered out.

Ramsey chuckled. "Yes, she did have a knack for getting all in our business. But I think we can safely say we wouldn't have wanted it any other way. I know Mom and Dad are smiling down on us today, happy for their baby girl."

He paused as if to compose himself before he continued, "And, Walker, she's yours now and I'm going to tell you the same thing I told Callum when he married Gemma, and Rico when he married Megan. You can't give her back. You asked for her, flaws and all, so deal with it."

Everyone laughed at that. Ramsey then raised his champagne glass higher. "To Walker and Bailey. May you have a long and wonderful marriage, and watch out for the bears." The attendees laughed again as they clicked their glasses before drinking their champagne.

Dillon then stepped up to stand beside Ramsey. The wedding had been held inside the beautiful garden club in downtown Denver. Riley's wife, Alpha, who was an event planner, had done her magic. The wedding theme had been From This Day Forward, and since it was Valentine's Day the colors had been red and white.

"No, I'm not giving Walker and Bailey another toast," Dillon said, grinning. "With so many members of the family gathered here together, I want to take this time to welcome our cousins, the Outlaws of Alaska. Your last names might be Outlaw but you proved just how much Westmoreland blood ran through your veins when you gave Bane and Crystal your protection when they needed it the most. And all of us thank you for it. Our great-grandfather Raphel would be proud. And that deserves another toast."

Crystal felt Bane's arms tighten around her waist. What Dillon had said was true. The Outlaws had come through for them during a very critical time. Their last names might be Outlaw, but they looked and carried themselves just like Westmorelands.

Later, she saw Dillon and Ramsey talking to Garth and Sloan and couldn't help but notice how the single

women at the wedding were checking them out. With all
the Denver Westmoreland males marked off the bachelor list, it seemed that the single ladies were considering the Outlaws as hopefuls. Evidently the thought of
moving to Alaska didn't dissuade them one bit.

"What's this I hear about the two of you moving
to Washington?" Senator Reggie Westmoreland approached to ask. He had his beautiful wife, Olivia, by
his side.

Bane smiled. "It will be just for a little while, after
Crystal graduates in May with her PhD. She will be
working at that lab in DC for six months and I was offered a position teaching SEAL recruits how to master a firearm."

"That's great! Libby and I will have to invite the two
of you over once you get settled."

Jess Outlaw walked up to join them. Because he
had been out on the campaign trail when they were in
Alaska, the first time Bane and Crystal had met him
had been when the Outlaws had joined the Westmorelands for Christmas.

"And I hope to see you soon in Washington, as well,"
Reggie said to Jess.

Jess smiled. "I hope so. The race is close and has
begun getting ugly."

"Been there before," Reggie said. "Hang in there and
stick to your principles."

Jess nodded. "Thanks for your advice, and thanks
so much for your endorsement."

A smile spread across Reggie's lips. "No thanks
needed. We are family. Besides, I reviewed your plat-
form, and it's a good one that could benefit the people
of your state. I think in the end they will see that."

"Let's hope so," Jess said.

A few moments later Crystal found herself alone with Bane. Coop was doing fine and had visited them in Westmoreland Country a few times. So had Nick, Flipper and Viper. Flipper had personally delivered to her the items that he and his brother had removed from her house before the fire.

She had gotten to know all of Bane's team members and thought they were swell guys. And she had met their wives, as well. But Flipper, Viper and Coop were single and swearing to stay that way. Since the three were extremely handsome men, she couldn't wait to see just for how long.

"Did I tell you today how much I love you?" Bane leaned down to ask her, whispering close to her ear.

"Yes," she said, smiling up at him. "But you can tell me again."

"Gladly. Crystal Gayle Westmoreland, I love you very much. With all my heart."

She reached up and caressed his cheek as she thought about all they'd endured over the years. A lot had changed, but the one thing that had remained constant had been their love. "And I love you, too, Bane. With all my heart."

And then they kissed, sealing their words and their love. Forever.

* * * * *

If you loved Bane's story,
pick up all the Westmoreland novels,
many now available in convenient box sets!

Volume 1
Brenda Jackson's THE WESTMORELAND SERIES
Books 1 to 5

DELANEY'S DESERT SHEIKH
A LITTLE DARE
THORN'S CHALLENGE
STONE COLD SURRENDER
RIDING THE STORM

Volume 2
Brenda Jackson's THE WESTMORELAND SERIES
Books 6 to 10

JARED'S COUNTERFEIT FIANCÉE
THE CHASE IS ON
THE DURANGO AFFAIR
IAN'S ULTIMATE GAMBLE
SEDUCTION, WESTMORELAND STYLE

Volume 3
Brenda Jackson's THE WESTMORELAND SERIES
Books 11 to 15

SPENCER'S FORBIDDEN PASSION
COLE'S RED-HOT PURSUIT
TAMING CLINT WESTMORELAND
QUADE'S BABIES
TALL, DARK...WESTMORELAND!

Volume 4
Brenda Jackson's THE WESTMORELAND SERIES
Books 16 to 20

WESTMORELAND'S WAY
HOT WESTMORELAND NIGHTS
WHAT A WESTMORELAND WANTS
A WIFE FOR A WESTMORELAND
THE PROPOSAL

Volume 5
Brenda Jackson's THE WESTMORELAND SERIES
Books 21 to 25

FEELING THE HEAT
TEXAS WILD
ONE WINTER'S NIGHT
ZANE
CANYON

And

STERN
THE REAL THING
THE SECRET AFFAIR
BREAKING BAILEY'S RULES

***

If you're on Twitter, tell us what you think of
Harlequin Desire! #harlequindesire

COMING NEXT MONTH FROM

⟨H⟩HARLEQUIN®
Desire

Available January 5, 2016

HDCNM1215

REQUEST YOUR FREE BOOKS!
2 FREE NOVELS PLUS 2 FREE GIFTS!

HARLEQUIN®

Desire

ALWAYS POWERFUL, PASSIONATE AND PROVOCATIVE

YES! Please send me 2 FREE Harlequin® Desire novels and my 2 FREE gifts (gifts are worth about $10). After receiving them, if I don't wish to receive any more books, I can return the shipping statement marked "cancel." If I don't cancel, I will receive 6 brand-new novels every month and be billed just $4.55 per book in the U.S. or $5.24 per book in Canada. That's a savings of at least 13% off the cover price! It's quite a bargain! Shipping and handling is just 50¢ per book in the U.S. and 75¢ per book in Canada.* I understand that accepting the 2 free books and gifts places me under no obligation to buy anything. I can always return a shipment and cancel at any time. Even if I never buy another book, the two free books and gifts are mine to keep forever.

225/326 HDN GH2P

Name	(PLEASE PRINT)

Address	Apt. #

City	State/Prov.	Zip/Postal Code

Signature (if under 18, a parent or guardian must sign)

Mail to the **Reader Service**:

IN U.S.A.: P.O. Box 1867, Buffalo, NY 14240-1867
IN CANADA: P.O. Box 609, Fort Erie, Ontario L2A 5X3

Want to try two free books from another line?
Call 1-800-873-8635 or visit www.ReaderService.com.

* Terms and prices subject to change without notice. Prices do not include applicable taxes. Sales tax applicable in N.Y. Canadian residents will be charged applicable taxes. Offer not valid in Quebec. This offer is limited to one order per household. Not valid for current subscribers to Harlequin Desire books. All orders subject to credit approval. Credit or debit balances in a customer's account(s) may be offset by any other outstanding balance owed by or to the customer. Please allow 4 to 6 weeks for delivery. Offer available while quantities last.

Your Privacy—The Reader Service is committed to protecting your privacy. Our Privacy Policy is available online at www.ReaderService.com or upon request from the Reader Service.

We make a portion of our mailing list available to reputable third parties that offer products we believe may interest you. If you prefer that we not exchange your name with third parties, or if you wish to clarify or modify your communication preferences, please visit us at www.ReaderService.com/consumerchoice or write to us at Reader Service Preference Service, P.O. Box 9062, Buffalo, NY 14240-9062. Include your complete name and address.

HD15

Kassandra fumbled for the remote, pushing every button
before she managed to turn off the TV.

But it was too late. She'd seen him. For the first time
since she'd walked out of his hospital room twenty-six
months ago. That had been the last time the world had
seen him, too. He'd dropped off the radar completely ever
since. Now her retinas burned with the image of Leonid
striding out of his imposing Fifth Avenue headquarters.

The man she'd known had been crackling with vitality,
a smile of whimsy and assurance always hovering on his
lips and sparkling in the depths of his eyes. This man
was totally detached, as if he was no longer part of the
world. Or as if it was beneath his notice. And there'd been
another change. The stalking swagger was gone. In its
place was a deliberate, almost menacing prowl.

This wasn't the man she'd known.

Or rather, the man she'd thought she'd known.

She'd long ago faced the fact that she'd known nothing
of him. Not before she'd been with him, or while they'd
been together, or after he'd shoved her away and vanished.

Kassandra had withdrawn from the world, too. She'd been pathetic enough to be literally sick with worry about him, to pine for him until she'd wasted away. Until she'd almost miscarried. That scare had finally jolted her to the one reality she'd been certain of. That she'd wanted that baby with everything in her and would never risk losing it. That day at the doctor's, she'd found out she wasn't carrying one baby, but two.

She'd reclaimed herself and her stability, had become even more successful career-wise, but most important, she'd become a mother to two perfect daughters. Eva and Zoya. She'd given them both names meaning life, as they'd given *her* new life.

Then Zorya had suddenly filled the news with a declaration of its intention to reinstate the monarchy. With every rapid development, foreboding had filled her. Even when she'd had no reason to think it would make Leonid resurface.

The doorbell rang.

It had become a ritual for her neighbor to come by and have a cup of tea so they could unwind together after their hectic days.

Rushing to the door, she opened it with a ready smile. "We should…"

Air clogged her lungs. All her nerves fired, short-circuiting her every muscle, especially her heart.

Leonid.

Right there. On her doorstep.

Turn your love of reading into rewards you'll love with

Harlequin My Rewards

**Join for FREE today at
www.HarlequinMyRewards.com**

Earn **FREE BOOKS** of your choice.

Experience **EXCLUSIVE OFFERS** and contests.

Enjoy **BOOK RECOMMENDATIONS**
selected just for you.

PLUS! Sign up now
and get **500** points
right away!

Earn
FREE
REWARDS
HarlequinMyRewards.com
Join
Today!

MYR16R

Love the Harlequin book you just read?

Your opinion matters.

Review this book on your favorite
book site, review site, blog or your own
social media properties and share
your opinion with other readers!

Be sure to connect with us at:
Harlequin.com/Newsletters
Facebook.com/HarlequinBooks
Twitter.com/HarlequinBooks

THE WORLD IS BETTER
WITH
Romance

Harlequin has everything from contemporary, passionate and heartwarming to suspenseful and inspirational stories.

Whatever your mood, we have a romance just for you!

Connect with us to find your next great read, special offers and more.

f /HarlequinBooks

🐦 @HarlequinBooks

www.HarlequinBlog.com

www.Harlequin.com/Newsletters